FILTHY CHRISTMAS

A VERY O'DONNELLY HOLIDAY!

A FIVE POINTS' CHRISTMAS NOVEL

SERENA AKEROYD

To my patrons,
This started as my love letter to you because you gave me the space to write this. Filthy Christmas wouldn't exist without you. So, thank you. Truly. I needed to see the O'Donnellys again and I could because of your support.
Much love and thanks to each of you

FOREWORD

I know, all right?

I know you want Stan. I know you want Maxim. I know. Trust me. 🤣

They're written! I pinky promise.

And they're coming next year.

But, first, here's my homage to the Feckers. Who I missed. Who I needed to reconnect with.

This is a slice of Fecker life that I'm pretty sure you needed in *your* lives too. I know I did.

Timeline-wise, FILTHY CHRISTMAS comes before Filthy Richer, after The Salvation Duet (Stan's duet,) but DURING Maxim and Victoria's story... You don't really need to know that, though, so, enjoy!

Triggers:

No elves were harmed during the making of this story. BUT some turkey basters were inserted in non-insertable areas so be warned.

Happy holidays from the O'Donnelly household to yours 🎅

Love,
Serena
xo

PLAYLIST

If you'd like to hear a curated soundtrack, with songs that are featured in the book, as well as songs that inspired it, then here's the link:

https://open.spotify.com/playlist/optV73heariwUUtmfLwuzf?si=66b3823f60e84ad4

THE CROSSOVER READING ORDER WITH THE SINNERS & VALENTINIS

FILTHY

FILTHY SINNER

NYX

LINK

FILTHY RICH

SIN

STEEL

FILTHY DARK

CRUZ

MAVERICK

FILTHY SEX

HAWK

FILTHY HOT

STORM

THE DON

THE LADY

FILTHY SECRET

REX

RACHEL

<u>FILTHY KING</u>
<u>FILTHY DISCIPLE</u>
<u>THE CONSIGLIERE</u>
<u>THE ORACLE</u>
<u>LODESTAR</u>
<u>SILENCED</u>
<u>END GAME</u>
WAITING GAME
THINGS LEFT UNSAID
COME BACK TO ME
>> FILTHY CHRISTMAS <<
<u>FILTHY RICHER</u>

ONE

"O'DONNELLYS ASSEMBLE!"

Star's hundred-decibel shout had me rubbing my temples. Both of them. Simultaneously. "For fuck's sake."

A malicious gleam appeared in her eyes. "Late night?"

I ignored her and, instead, watched as the mass of women and children's heads turned to face my former BFF.

I swore—if she weren't so handy with a knife, I'd make her regret that whistle.

Of course, the mischief I literally made tumbled into my lap, her inquisitive eyes—Aidan's eyes—switching between her aunt and me. Her little, pointy elbows and knees didn't give a damn that they dug into soft, squishy bits as she plunked herself into a prime spot for the gossip.

Nosy.

Third totally inherited that from me.

As I hugged her to me, enjoying the faint traces of baby powder and milk, I refused to cry. Because if I did, it scared her, and I never wanted her to be scared.

Plus, there was no need to cry.

So what if Aidan had frozen me out last night?! Just because he'd never done that before, ever, well, so. What?!

Grabbing Cameron's hands before he could snag another cinnamon roll, Aela blew out a puff of hair that clung to her brow. "What's going on, Star? I told you not to do that. It drives me insane. Also, we're not dogs."

"That's what she said," Star chirped. "Anyway, I have good news."

Eyes wide, Aoife sank back into the armchair. "No way. You did it?"

Star smirked. "I did. Just call me God. Miracle maker par excellence."

"In your dreams." I hooted. "Your ego is plenty big enough."

"Did what?" Camille inserted, dragging Jake onto her lap, preventing a head-on collision with a tea tray. "What miracles did you make happen?"

"I managed to *convince* Conor that Lena needs a break over the holidays. She and Paddy are going on a martyrs' honeymoon."

I took a deep sip of coffee. "Do I even want to know what that means?"

Inessa gawked at Star. "They're married?"

"Nope. But you just watch her come back with a ring on her finger."

While Inessa's nose scrunched, I chuckled more at Star's glare. "Her review on your stuffing still stings, huh? *All* these years later. How precious."

"Fucking bitch thinks she knows everything," Star muttered in an aside.

"I heard that," Kat sang, then waggled her fingers in front of her mother. "Swear jar. You promised."

"She used two curse words."

Kat beamed at me. "Thanks, Aunty S!"

"You're welcome, honey." Pressing my cheek to Aidan's, I sank back in my own armchair as Star coughed up twenty bucks. "Jesus, that's how much two curse words cost nowadays?"

"You don't want to know what the tooth fairy charges." Aoife's gaze turned concerned. "Are you okay, Savvie? You look a little…"

"Like dogshit?"

"Another ten bucks for the jar, Kat," I yelled, then gestured at Third. "Little ears!"

Of course, Star's potty mouth wouldn't be vanquished. "*Motherfucker.*"

"She owes twenty now."

Kat made an appearance, hand outstretched. She shoved the twenty into a purse she tucked into her low-slung jeans then leaned down and whispered in my ear, "I'll cut you in if you keep this up, Aunty S! You're really good at pumping Mom for the dough."

I hid a smile as she pecked Third on the cheek, not caring that she had chocolate frosting liberally coating her. "Where are the proceeds going?"

"A trip to Lapland."

"Lapland, huh?"

"Oh, yes. Now that I can legally travel out of the country, I want to see the reindeer."

Star shot her daughter an unimpressed look. "And I told her she can go upstate and see those."

"That isn't the same and you know it. Plus, I want us all to experience the northern lights."

"You can see those in North America."

"Not. The. Same."

"Has nothing to do with St. Nick, huh?" I teased, just to watch her blush.

She'd grown oddly mature in the last couple years. Childhood didn't set well on her shoulders, but neither did adulthood. I'd experienced the horrors of the teen years with my sisters, so I had a point of reference—Kat was nothing like them.

"I'm too old for Santa."

Star immediately scowled. "No, you're not, and if those little shits in school are—"

"Ten bucks, please!" Kat held out her hand. "I'm running out of time, Aunty S. So any help is appreciated," she told me sweetly before grabbing Third around the waist, then stomping over to the other side of the room where the kids gathered.

Shay graced us with his presence for once, and the fact that Kat was more interested in catching her mother out than hanging all over him spoke of her desperation for a trip to Lapland.

The mania of an afternoon with the sisters-in-law never changed, apart from at this time of the year—the holidays had come back around. Which meant chaos had escaped the building to spare itself a headache. Thanksgiving. Check. We were officially on Christmas watch.

"How did you 'convince' Conor to 'convince' Lena that she needs a break?" Aela bit into her macaron.

"Paddy helped me."

"Paddy wanted a vacay too, huh?" Aoife teased.

"Yup." She snagged one of the club sandwiches from a silver tray and stacked three on top of each other. "I don't think he reckoned on pilgrimage sites in Europe. Probably figured it'd be Boca Raton, but them's the cards."

Inessa sipped her mint tea. "Knowing him, he'll turn it into a pub crawl."

"I'd pay to go with him. He has a fab eye for a good pub." I stole one of the sandwiches from Star's hands. "So, when are we free of the wicked witch?"

"The twenty-third—"

"Meeee?!" my precocious child shrieked with glee.

Aoife tutted. "Baby Aidan, what did we tell you about listening in?"

Third sang, "I'm doing what my daddy taught me. Information is queen!"

While Aoife facepalmed, I directed with a laugh, "Keep watching your show, sweetie."

Snorting, Star continued, "She wants a pre-holiday dinner. That's the payment."

"So close to Christmas?"

"Since when did Lena care about being irrelevant?"

I hid a smirk. "What's a martyrs' honeymoon, anyway?"

"Fuck if I know. Lots of dead people shit to see in Europe, I guess."

Camille groaned. "Star!"

A wicked glint appeared in her eyes.

"Wait." I winced. "Who's cooking?"

Please not me. It was Finn and Aoife's turn to host Christmas, but with their 'Lena' situation and Aidan and I due to host next year...

"She is, of course. At her damn place in her own damn kitchen."

Inessa bit her lip. "Have you cleared this with the guys?"

"Look, *Nessie*, you might need to hold Eoghan's dick when he pisses, but I let Conor do his own housekeeping. He's a big boy and can arrange shit without me overseeing stuff. Don't forget, he thinks this gift is *his* idea."

Camille cackled at Inessa's wide, horrified eyes. "I don't think she's seen Eoghan pee yet."

"Why would I want to?" my youngest sister-in-law sputtered. "I mean, of course I've been in the bathroom when... but I don't go in and talk to him!"

"She's young still," Aela mocked with a wicked glint. "Just wait until you pop out your first kid. If you're dealing with a diaper blowout, you won't give a damn if he's peeing or not."

Inessa's nose scrunched again. "How did we get onto this subject?! I'd rather talk about the stuffing wars of '23 than this!"

Star took an overly large bite of her sandwich. "I expect good gifts this year for my sacrifice."

I jeered, "What sacrifice?"

"Hey, Conor took some persuading."

"I bet." I rolled my eyes. "Do you think I was born yesterday?"

Aela pursed her lips. "You raise a valid point, Star—"

"Don't I always?"

"—we need to talk about gifts."

"Secret Santa?" Aoife offered when I groaned. "Genuinely, Savvie, are you feeling okay?"

"I'm fine."

"You look under the weather."

"Can't talk about it," I groused.

"Or don't want to?" Star folded her arms across her chest. "Come on. You'll feel better. You've been like a bear with a sore paw since we arrived. Only two orgasms last night, not your usual half dozen?"

"Star!" Camille tutted then her head tipped to the side as she examined me. "Aoife's right. You do look pale."

My shoulders slumped. "I didn't sleep well. Aidan and I argued last night."

"So? You're always bickering."

"Yes, Star," I hissed. "But this time, I slept in the guest room and he wasn't there at breakfast this morning."

If I didn't have my sisters' attention by that point, that earned it—each of their heads whipped around to face me.

"You slept in the guest room?!" Inessa gasped like I'd told her Aidan had burned down *another* church.

"I did."

Star's tone promised a brutal butchering. "Do I need to get my special scissors out?"

Ah, there was my sister from another mister—reassuring and terrifying me in one fell swoop. "No. I still like his penis fully functioning, Star."

"So, why did you not sleep in your bedroom? I thought you guys didn't do that?"

"We don't." Aoife's question had me swallowing down tears.

"Holy shit, is she crying?" Inessa asked Camille.

My hand shook as I trickled it along my lower lash. "It's fine. We'll hash it out later."

"No, it's not. Is there anything we can do? I could get Finn to shake some sense into him? Aidan actually listens to him." Aoife leaned over to pat my hand. "Or do you want some brownies?"

I sucked in my bottom lip. "Your brownies *do* fix everything."

Aoife snagged her phone. "I'll have some delivered."

"Thanks, Eef. You're the best."

"I try." She winked at me before tapping out a couple messages to someone on her staff, I presumed. "Okay, so what's going on?"

"I'm writing an article and he won't help me." There, that was oblique enough.

"What do you need help with? Can I do anything?" Star dragged the tray of club sandwich triangles and plopped it on my knee. "In the meantime, eat your feelings or I *will* get out my special scissors. You know I won't let him make you cry. Remember Jersey Vorul."

"Love you too." Ignoring her scowl, I grabbed a sandwich. "There's a place in Lower Manhattan. I've heard rumors about them hosting fights there."

"Wait," Inessa butted in. "Who's Jersey Vorul?"

"Singer. He toured with Daddy."

Star cackled.

"Oh boy, what happened?" Camille inquired with a smile.

Admittedly, that cackle was contagious.

"That tour was his big break. Then he came onto Vana and I ruined his career."

"Ouch. Intense," Aoife muttered, eyes wide.

"I was thirteen."

Her tone did a 180. "That asshole!"

"That's why you've never heard of him," I tacked on dryly. "Star did what Star does best."

Smugly, Star demanded, "What kind of fights in Lower Manhattan?"

"Animal fights."

Everyone, apart from Star, gasped. She just asked, "I can trawl for info?"

I shook my head. "It's fine."

"Hardly! You slept in separate bedrooms," Aela pointed out. "So, what led to that?"

"I'm not even sure. He said he'd know if any faction was hosting those kinds of events, and then things just spiraled."

"Spiraled, how?" Aoife cleared her throat. "Not going to lie, Savvie, you two are usually the least argue-y of the bunch."

Camille took a dainty bite of a scone. "Argue-y?"

"What?! You know I'm right."

"That's because Savannah thinks with her clitoris," Star intoned.

"Maybe." I inhaled another sandwich. "Look, I'm okay. I just woke up with a headache."

"Because you went to sleep crying?"

"Mostly out of exasperation. He didn't even raise his damn voice." I shuddered. "That's so fucking hot too."

"Only because your mom and dad blow hot during arguments." Star clucked her tongue. "So, you're going to overdose on carbs and then...?"

"Go home."

"Where are you sleeping?"

"Depends."

"On?" Camille prompted.

"I don't know."

"Jesus, you guys really *don't* argue, do you?" Aela laughed, but it wasn't mean, just perplexed. "I don't know how you can't. They're all so fucking stubborn."

"Did I hear a swear word?" Kat hollered.

"Not from me!" Star yelled back then added, "Brat!"

"Did someone say my name in vain?" Victoria chimed in.

"Not you," Star groused. "*My* brat. And that isn't a curse word, Kat, so keep your nose *and* your hands out of my wallet."

My lips twitched into a smile. "Just take her to Lapland already, Scrooge."

"I will, but there's no point until after school breaks. Then we'll head over for a couple days, but don't tell her that. She can pay for her own damn ticket."

"This is your way of teaching her fiscal responsibility?" Aoife sputtered.

"Duh."

"You could just ask me to get her an afternoon job in one of the bakeries?"

"Nah. Conor would insist on a protective detail, which she'd hate, so I'd have to sit in there, and my butt has doubled in size since we got together. I still need to kick ass, and I won't be able to if I'm surrounded by your fucking food—" She jumped when Kat popped up from out of nowhere. "Fuck's sake, Kat! Where the hell did you come from, demon teenager? Which, before you ask, is infinitely worse than demon child!"

"Pay up!" Kat's gleeful voice earned her a huff, but Star handed over a twenty. "Hey, you used 'hell' and 'ass' too."

"Since when are they curses?"

"Since forever."

Star pulled a face when her wallet turned up empty. "I'll have to owe you."

"No fair!"

"You stripped me of cash, kid."

"Don't worry. We can stop at the bank before we go home, Star," Kat chirped as she walked over to the TV.

With my teacup in front of my mouth, I sang, "You're creating a monster."

"Precisely. I want her to be a monster. She won't get hurt that way. I love destroying the Jersey Voruls of this world, but Conor made me promise not to kill people."

"Again? Isn't that like the fourth promise?" Inessa joked.

"Fifth. What can I say? Some cunts," Star whispered, "just need to die. Speaking of which... Aidan. You'd better call me tonight if you're still arguing when you get back."

"I will. Last night came out of left field, but I like him alive, Star," I reminded her. "Okay, so, gifts? Secret Santa?"

"This year... we could make each other presents."

Only Camille and Aoife didn't groan at Aela's suggestion.

"Do I look like the sort of person who macramés?" Star demanded.

"I know you started crocheting, Star. Don't bullshit me," Aela countered.

"You crochet?!"

Star glowered at her boots. "Conor suggested it. Said it might be relaxing."

"Didn't work, did it?"

"Fuck you," she said sweetly.

"Kat! Your mother owes you another ten." As my minx of a niece wooted over by the TV, I continued, "I don't make stuff."

"Well, you can try."

"I pity the person I pick then."

Aoife just smiled. "I think it's a great idea, Aela. So, we're in agreement?"

"Yeah, I'd be down," Camille agreed.

Star scratched her nose. "Fine."

Inessa shrugged. "If that's what everyone wants to do."

Aela smirked. "Just FYI, I'm not going to make you something you can sell later."

"No fair," Star chimed in with a grin.

Groaning, I grouched, "Okay. Homemade, it is."

IN THE MOODY light of a grim day in New York, it was pure chance that it caught my eye.

It—a sharp gleam reflecting off glass.

In a city of skyscrapers, that kind of thing happened on the regular.

But this was different. Glass on a rooftop? Nope. On the edge, where there were no windows at all? Nah.

My husband had trained me too well to—

"Nessa?"

I jumped. "Yes?"

Camille shoved a bag at me. "Pick out a name."

Grimacing, I stared at the empty chips bag. "This was the best we could do?"

"Don't be a baby."

Nose wrinkling, I plucked a small piece of paper out, trying to avoid the Cheeto dust that coated Jake, Niall, and Cameron's lips— clearly the donors of the bag in question.

Another sharp glint of light reflected off the back wall before I could read the name and had me whipping around to look out the window again.

"You okay?"

"Yeah, I'm fine, Camille."

"Who'd you get?"

"Huh?"

She huffed. "Are you listening?"

"Not really."

"Secret Santa," she protested. "Who did you get?"

"Isn't the secret part the whole point?"

That earned me a second huff and she flounced off, the Cheeto bag in her hand as she shoved it at our sisters-in-law and waited for them to make their selections.

As the others talked about their crafting plans for Secret Santa, I reached for my phone and typed:

> Me: You'd better not be where I think you are

I didn't have to wait long for a reply.

> Eoghan: Where do you think I might be?

> Me: Somewhere you shouldn't be.

> Eoghan: I doubt I'm where you think I am

> Me: Oh, I think you're exactly where you are

My lips pursed as I slipped out of the hotel suite's main room and drifted into the bedroom, barely avoiding a convergence of the three greatest terrors in NYC—Star's Niall, Savvie's Third, and my other nephew twice over, Roman.

I steered clear of the windows because if my husband *was* watching me, I didn't want to freak him out.

Eoghan said that his greatest enemy were windows.

I knew he had nightmares about them. To be specific, me standing in front of them. Getting shot by an enemy.

The minutiae of my passing hadn't come up in regular conversation before my marriage. Now, it happened whenever he stirred in the middle of the night, his subconscious fears driving him to hold me close. To never let me go.

A love like Eoghan's wasn't something I ever thought I'd experience.

It probably spoke of my fucked-up upbringing that it didn't suffocate me. At all. It was just... *him*. And I craved him as much as he needed me.

Eoghan: What are you doing?

When I perched on the bed, I knew he'd be able to see me. Undoubtedly, he'd followed me with his scope.

Rather than answer, I snagged the top button of my blouse and popped it open.

Then another.

And another.

My tits were sore so I hadn't bothered with a bra—that meant he got the *whole* show.

I had no intention of following through, but he didn't need to know that, did he?

Instead, I gently rubbed my nipple, trailed my fingers over the swell, keeping it slow and easy because they ached like a SOB today.

Eoghan: Well? What are you doing?

I licked a finger and circled my nipple.

Eoghan: Seriously, I have no idea where you are

I leaned forward, pushing them together and—

> Eoghan: I know you're reading my messages

I let my hand sweep over my abdomen, allowed my fingers to swirl around my navel before I approached the waistband of my pencil skirt.

> Eoghan: FINE

I smirked.

> Eoghan: I was just securing the area
>
> Eoghan: That's it
>
> Eoghan: I'll go home
>
> Eoghan: I'll see you later
>
> Eoghan: I won't watch anymore
>
> Eoghan: I won't
>
> Eoghan: You can button your blouse up. Do you know those windows aren't reflective?!
>
> Eoghan: Where's your bra anyway?
>
> Eoghan: Inessa!

I arched a brow.

> Eoghan: Fuck
>
> Eoghan: I'm going
>
> Eoghan: For real.
>
> Eoghan: This time

I remained there, perching on the bedside for a good five minutes.

Another glint sparked in the distance.

My cell buzzed.

"What are you trying to do me?!"

"Torture you, of course. What else?"

He groaned. "I'm not even there anymore."

"Liar. I saw your scope."

"Fuck. Winter sun drives me crazy. And I accounted for that too. Just not how goddamn long you'd be hanging out today." He heaved a sigh. "You look gorgeous. But genuinely, where's your bra?"

"I didn't wear one today."

His hiss had me smiling. "Shit. You're on your period, aren't you?"

No. "Yes." I wasn't ready to talk about this yet.

"That means you really were torturing me!"

"I won't reward stalking like it's good behavior." Then, I conceded, "Even if it's 'protective' stalking. I'm hanging out with my sisters-in-law, Eoghan. We talk about things that have nothing to do with the boys."

"I can't read lips."

"I don't believe you."

"I'm wounded."

I hooted. "You sound like it."

"I am! We used to have so much trust between us."

"Then you started following me around the city." I stood up, moved closer to the window, but remained half-tucked behind the drapes. I didn't like that the fabric touched my naked breasts and the scratchy silk sent a shiver down my spine.

"I can't decide if this is encouragement or not." He paused. "It'd be wrong to jack off, wouldn't it?"

"Isn't it too cold for that?"

"I've jacked off in colder places. The boner after... never mind."

"Good to know," I drawled as I toyed with one of my nipples.

We'd be bringing that topic up again.

"Fuck. Your tits are so gorgeous. I had no way of knowing that I'd marry a woman who put a *Sports Illustrated* model's to shame. Kid Eoghan is so cheering me on right now."

"You're not getting in my panties."

"I don't mind a bit of blood."

"No, but I do."

"I'll clean up the bed."

"Last time looked like a scene from a horror movie!"

"How about the shower?"

Even though I wasn't menstruating, I still pondered the suggestion. "Maybe. If the cramps come back."

"Want me to pick up some gingerbread popcorn?"

"Don't lie. You'll wait until I leave and then follow me home."

"I could join you in the car."

"That'd be the eco-friendly option," I agreed. "But I'm going with Camille, Star, and Savvie to Aoife's bakery on Fifth with the kids."

It wasn't a lie. But my doctor's office was around the block...

"Who did you pick for Secret Santa?"

"I knew you could lip-read!"

"Who?"

"That'd be telling."

"What are you making them?"

My gaze tripped over one of the stores in the building he used as a prop. It'd have been so much damn easier to head in there and buy a gift. But noooo, crafting. Ugh.

"I don't know." Wistfully, I looked at the ice-skating rink where kids and adults alike were whirling around an oversized Christmas tree that glittered in the darkening sky. "I'm not the best at making shit."

"I can sew."

Well, that put my attention purely back on him. "*You* can sew?!"

"Don't be sexist."

"I'm not! My gast is fully flabbered! What can you sew?"

"Mostly open wounds." He ignored my groan. "But Ma had a dress shop when we were young. I had to go there after school. Used to play with the needles. And scissors, actually."

"Better than knives."

"For the eyes, they are."

"I don't want to know."

"Probably not."

"What would you make?"

"Hey, I'm just offering to put together whatever you decide."

"In exchange for phone sex?" I hummed. "You got your dick in your hand?"

"Maybe."

"Is it a Popsicle yet?"

He chuckled. "This double-talk always gets me in the mood."

Just to hear him moan, I cupped my breast. "You like that I don't let you get away with shit."

It'd taken me a couple of years to get into the swing of things, but no O'Donnelly appreciated a pushover.

"I fucking love it."

"As much as sliding your cock into my pussy?"

"No. Nothing beats that. Nothing."

And *I* fucking loved that he was croaking already.

Nothing empowered me more than knowing that I could bring a man like Eoghan O'Donnelly to this state with a jiggle of my tits and a few dirty words.

"Nothing? How about when I suck you off? Get your cock all wet and stare into your eyes when I take you to the back of my throat."

"God, that's high up there."

Cursing my exhibitionist nature, I bit my lip.

Of course, he spotted it. "You wet, sweetheart?"

"You know I am."

"You're always horny when you get your period. I could meet you in a hotel suite. You wouldn't have to clean up—"

"Eoghan! I'm not having some poor housekeeper deal with that mess!"

"But you know you'd feel so much fucking better. I'd get you off, babe. Make you all relaxed, then I'd slide into you and take such care of you. I only want you to feel good."

My jaw worked.

Damn if I didn't want that too. Especially with how nauseated I'd felt recently.

Still, I teased, "Maybe I'd want you to be rough with me. Pin me to the bed and fuck me so hard the bed shook."

"Face down or eyes on me?" he rumbled.

"Eyes on you," I breathed. "Arms over my head. Your legs locking me in place, hands holding me down."

"Ohh, you'd want to be restrained, would you? Want me to not let you go until I'd finished."

"Fuck, yeah. Until you'd pumped me full of your cum."

"I'd watch it slide out of you just so that I could stuff it back inside."

"You want to breed me, baby?"

I heard his guttural curse even if he muttered it under his breath.

"You want the whole world to know I'm yours? That you claimed me?"

"The world knows you're mine," he snarled. "Only mine."

"Always," I whispered.

"I'm so fucking close, Inessa. How do you do this to me every time—" He grunted. "God. Damn. It. Wish I were fucking you. Holding you down and making you take every inch of this cock that's so close to exploding because of you. Nobody gets me like this. Nobody, Inessa."

Cheeks flushing, I swallowed. "No one gets me wet like you, Eoghan. I'm crazy about you. Don't you know? I want you all the time. I want you to come so bad. I wish I could see. I'd let you come all over my tits and I'd let you rub it in. Then I'd walk around the whole day with you on me—"

"Fuck!" he roared in my ear. Low breaths sounded next, heavy and deep as he panted through his orgasm.

I squirmed, turned on but determined not to do anything about it. Still, his reaction was a great anxiety killer.

"You're such a good fucking girl for me. Later, I'm going to fill the bath for you. Gonna throw in all that stinky shit you adore and then I'll climb into it too and sit you on my cock until you get off. You can't complain about cleanup if we're in the bathroom. You like the idea of that, baby?"

"You know I do." I closed my eyes, easily able to imagine the scene he set. "But I'm out of my favorite stinky shit."

He grunted.

"*And* you ate the last of my Dairy Milk stash *and* gingerbread popcorn."

"Fine."

I twirled a strand of hair around my finger. "I'll see you at home?"

"How long are you guys going to be?"

"I don't know, Eoghan. What happens during afternoon tea, stays at afternoon tea. That's the deal."

"That isn't as threatening as you think it is."

"I don't think it's threatening at all."

He snorted. "Do you need anything else from the store? You good for tampons?"

"Eoghan!"

His goddamn obsession with my body—I'd had to throw away so many tampons recently!

"What? For someone who goes through this every month, you run out of this shit all the time. I don't know why you don't use one of those cups. I'll put it in for you—"

"Eoghan O'Donnelly! You shut your mouth! I'm not letting you do that!"

"Why not? I've seen you puke."

"Because I was ill. That was an aberration."

He barked out a laugh. "I should pee in front of you just to get you used to it. Aela's right—"

"Aela is wrong, Mr. Lip-reader. My father never saw my mom without makeup. Even if she was sick, she used to wear it."

"Oh, babe, that's so fucking sad. Don't you see that? I don't need you to look perfect. That isn't you. That's not my Inessa."

I propped my phone between my shoulder and ear as I buttoned up my blouse. "I like to look nice for you."

"And I just need you to look like you. When you're in the gym, hot and sweaty, you're so fucking sexy—"

"Shut up!"

"You blushing? Daaamn. I definitely need to get you in the bath ASAP. Let you burn it off."

"Eoghan," I whined, but of course, the hunter in him knew he had me right where he wanted me.

"I just know that pretty little pussy is so hungry for me." When I huffed, he drawled, "You go and play with your friends, and I'll get provisions. Shall I bring home takeout?"

I really wanted sushi, but not until the doctor confirmed my suspicions. "Pizza from that place on 4th?"

"Sounds good to me. We can watch that damn show you've been talking about too. Braxton Hall?"

I hid a smile. "*Maxton Hall.* You're too good to me, Eoghan."

"Baby, you're the one who just talked me off while I watched you through a sniper-rifle scope on a rooftop. *You* are too good to *me.*"

"You wouldn't be you if you weren't weird."

Eoghan laughed. "Thank fuck you think so. Okay, I'm heading off. Text me if you think of something you want."

Touched, as always, by his thoughtfulness, I breathed, "I just want you."

Then I cut the call.

Turning away from the window, I began the walk of shame to the living room.

I knew he'd come with me if I asked him to, but I also knew he'd freak out. I wanted to delay that until I had time to process the situation.

I'd been an aunt for a long time now.

Just never a mother.

My cell buzzed.

> Eoghan: I always want you.
>
> Eoghan: I love you, Inessa.
>
> Eoghan: YOU.

Because I knew he meant it, I opened up my camera, said, "I love you too," as I filmed it, then I blew him a kiss.

When I returned to the living room after I'd sent it over, Camille caught my eye. I flared mine at her, silently pleading with her to leave my extended absence alone, and she just smiled.

Aoife, however, grinned at me.

I bit my lip then headed over to the club sandwiches that Savannah and Star were hoarding.

Suddenly, with my nerves abated, I had quite the appetite...

THREE

IT TOOK me entering the kitchen to realize my kiddo was sitting at the table in the complete dark.

"What are you doing, baby?"

Shay glowered at me over his shoulder. Whether that was because I switched on the under-counter lighting or— "Baby?! Really?"

Ah.

I chivvied, "You'll always be my love bug."

He gagged, but I saw the sparkle in his eye. "You're lucky I love you."

"Don't I know it." My tone was light as I brushed my fingers through his hair before settling my hand at the center of his back. Like usual, he wriggled his shoulders and released a sigh at the simple touch. "What's with the scowl anyway?"

"I wasn't scowling."

"Sure you were." I peered at his screen, unsurprised when he slammed it down before I could catch much more of a glimpse than a blank document and a cursor that tolled like a death knell. "No inspiration, huh?"

He sucked in a breath through his teeth. "Why can you always read me like a book?"

"Because we're cut from the same cloth." Wishing I could make this better, I pressed a kiss to his temple. "You need help with this essay, just tell me."

"Victoria's already finished her term papers," he complained. "She didn't even really want to attend Oakwood, and she keeps up with the work like a boss. Me? Even though I'm not, it's as if I'm slacking all the time. I know she only chose Oakwood so we can be together."

An amused smile curved my lips. "She's a sociopath."

"Mom!"

"She is. I'm telling you."

"Her attending the same college as me does not a sociopath make."

"There are many, many reasons that I know I'm right..." Like the fact that the head of the Russian faction routinely sent her goddamn severed body parts and Victoria remained as chirpy as ever. No therapy required. "...but the fact she got her term papers finished this early is definitely sociopathic."

"You're surrounded by enough that you'd know." Declan strolled into the kitchen with that swagger of his, which made me melt.

It helped that he had Cameron on his hip.

What could I say?

Declan and I reproduced to perfection.

Honestly, our kids were better than my works of art. And being surrounded by my family, in our kitchen, in our *home* never stopped giving me the squigglies.

For so long, what we had would have been an impossibility. Now, it was my life. My normal.

Until Shay departed for college, of course.

He was only here to help me decorate the tree and he'd gotten sideswiped by a professor changing the deadline on a term paper.

"Victoria isn't a sociopath." Shay sniffed. "If anything, she's a psychopath."

Though I hooted out a laugh at his surprise concession, Declan frowned. "What makes you say that?"

"She's a headcase, Dad. She might look like butter doesn't melt—"

"I will never understand that saying."

Ever patient, Shay explained, "It means her perceived innocence hides a thousand sins."

"What kind of sins? Sins that Brennan needs to cover up?"

"Not yet," Shay intoned grimly, but his smirk only widened as his father's eyes bugged. "I'm teasing. She isn't a psycho. Plus, she has Maxim for that now."

I shuddered. "She's something with a -pathic. That we can agree on. But I'm glad. You need someone to keep you out of trouble. Your heart's too big."

"Mom!"

"It is. You want to be the president, baby. Not because you'll be one of the most powerful men in the world, but because you want to make changes for the good of all. That says a lot about you, but mostly that you need someone to watch your back."

It had taken some time for me to understand the relationship Shay and Victoria, Inessa and Camille's baby sister, shared.

I'd caught them kissing once—not that they'd seen me snooping. But I'd heard their conversation. It was nothing like Dec and I shared after a make-out session. Be it now or twenty years ago. It had been like a lecture. Shay asking her if he should curl his tongue or if he'd been too eager. Her asking if it'd always be so *wet*.

Kissing lessons aside, I knew there was nothing sexual about their relationship. They were just friends. The best kind.

Honestly, their closeness relieved me.

Now that Victoria was married to Maxim Lyanov, that friendship would provide extra padding that'd ensure Shay's safety.

Victoria would *never* let anyone hurt Shay.

I had faith in that even if I had no faith in a man who thought decapitated heads were appropriate holiday gifts.

Shay's cheeks puffed out when Dec asked, "What's the problem? Why are we talking about Victoria anyway?"

"She's finished her term papers and is sliding into Christmas break with *no* homework."

Declan pulled a face. "I thought you had too."

"No," Shay mourned. "I've never been behind in my life. This sucks. I don't think anything could be worse—"

"Worse than spiders, Shay Shay?" Cameron mumbled sleepily from his position on his dad's lap after the very exciting playdate with the kids *and* a visit to Aunt Eef's bakery for brownies.

"Worse than spiders, little man."

"Atomic ones?"

"Yeah, buddy." Shay gave him a gentle noogie. "Ten times worse."

Cameron yawned. "Daddy's good at killing spiders. Maybe he can help."

"Not *atomic* ones."

A little hand patted Dec's chest. "Can't be good at everything, Daddy."

With my heart in a meltdown at the overload of cuteness, I murmured, "Want Daddy to read you a bedtime story, Cam?"

He nodded. "Long one."

"Think I can manage that." Declan ambled to his feet but clapped Shay on the shoulder. "You got this, son. And if Oakwood doesn't drool over every word you deign to write in these damn term papers, then it's not the right college for you."

Our son grimaced, but I caught his eye before he could back-talk, so he just muttered, "Thanks, Dad."

Once Dec was out of the kitchen, I soothed, "He means well."

Shay's expression tightened but he nodded. "I know."

"And he isn't dismissing your goals—"

"Mom. I *know*."

"Good." I released a relieved breath. Shay and his dad got along great, but we'd gone through several scholastic arguments that cropped up from time to time. Declan was no academic, and Shay, for all his dreams and current issues with the workload, loved his studies. "Don't sit here too long psyching yourself out, Shay. It won't help you get the work done."

"Why did he have to change the deadline? That should be against the law."

"You're overthinking this. You're a pro at essays. Just chill out—"

"This matters."

His fierce tone had me sighing. "I know. And I know you have a twenty-year plan and everything hinges on that, and sucking at Oakwood would be a disaster, but if you let the pressure hit now, then quite frankly, your plan's fucked."

His lips twisted into a grin. "Kat's still collecting. I can give her ten bucks if you want."

Now *that* was a relationship that concerned me.

Kat had the power to hurt Shay in a way I didn't think she understood yet.

Still, that was a conversation for another day, maybe a-never day, so I stuck out my tongue as I clambered to my feet and headed over to the refrigerator. "I have decorations to set up."

He glanced at the can in my hand once I rustled through the contents. "Time for the hard stuff."

"God, yes."

Before I reached the kitchen door, he called out, "Remember that swear jar we had when I was thirteen?"

"And you were cursing like a trooper? Yup."

So that's where Kat had gotten her idea.

"What did the money go toward again?"

"Unlike Kat, I didn't charge you ten dollars a swear word," I reminded him. "But I think we bought a laptop with the proceeds."

He stared at me from over his shoulder. "You really are the best, Mom."

I blew him a kiss. "You make it easy, kiddo."

Leaving him to stress out and knowing that I couldn't help his procrastination/writer's block, I strode into the living room where Declan had dumped the bins of Christmas decorations earlier.

Our deal was that he had to source the tree and put it in the corner beside the TV, help me pack up the ornaments once the holidays were over, and figure out storage for the many, many containers.

I had to decorate because, in his words, "my creative eye turned me into the Grinch."

Overwhelmed by the city of boxes, I hissed under my breath, "That still makes no sense."

To me, at least.

Shay had backed up his dad but, like the brave soul he was, always offered to help. Until homework got in the way, which left me alone with the gargantuan task ahead.

Popping my tab on the cocktail in a can, I took a sip of the vodka mule and tugged off the first lid.

Maybe it was luck that saw me uncovering ornaments Shay and I had bought on our travels. Each one a memory that let me reminisce about his childhood without bawling now that my baby was fully grown.

My lips quirked into a broad smile as I uncovered the little leprechaun with a Santa's hat he'd insisted we buy in a Tesco's in County Kerry one year, then the miniature cuckoo clock we'd found in the Schwarzwald.

I didn't even realize Dec was watching me sort out the ornaments until he asked, "What's the story with that one? Haven't seen it before."

I found him slouched on the sofa, a pensive expression etched into the lines of his face that I wanted to erase. "It's a kookaburra. We were in Melbourne one year. There's a market just outside the city. They sold all kinds of foods—it was the first time I convinced him to try a chicken and leek pie. Shay refused to eat anything white."

Dec's brows lifted but he laughed. "He wouldn't eat *anything* white?!"

"Nope." My smile deepened as I trekked through the boxes to reach the sofa so I could perch on his lap. "We've been lucky with Cameron so far. He's like a vacuum cleaner. Eats anything. Shay went through phases. The 'nothing white' one sucked. I've never known a kid to prefer brown bread to white, but Shay wouldn't touch it. For almost a year!"

"A *whole* year?!"

"I don't even know how I convinced him to eat the pie actually." My gaze turned distant. "Did he want to try vanilla ice cream? Maybe. I think I said he could have that if he tried what I'd picked. Anyway, the pie broke him down."

"That good?"

"We went back to that damn market three more times—he wouldn't eat anything else for a week!"

Eyes soft, he slotted his arms around my waist. "What were you doing in Australia?"

"A portrait. For this asshole sheep farmer. We had to stay at his station and, while his wife was a hoot, it sucked. As a treat, once the commission was over, I took Shay to Melbourne and we chilled out there for a couple weeks." I stroked my fingers over the ornament. "He had to settle for a kookaburra because he couldn't find any bin chickens."

"Any what now?"

"Bin chickens." I smirked.

"Like trash pandas?"

"Of the avian variety. They're these crazy-looking birds that eat out of bins. Australians have a love/hate relationship with them, but Shay adored them." I popped my hip so that I could snag my cell from my back pocket. A quick search and I showed him a picture.

"Holy shit, they look like something from Ancient Egypt."

"Trust me. They have the presence of an Egyptian god. I just bet Anubis was seeing them on the side." I gently patted the ornament. "You can always ask, you know?"

His eyes suddenly fixated on the barren tree. "Ask what?"

I huffed and snagged his chin so he had to look at me. "About the times we were together, just him and me. You don't need a Christmas ornament to trigger a conversation. I'm an open book with you. You know that."

"Sometimes…"

"Sometimes?" I gently prodded when his Adam's apple bobbed.

"Sometimes it's hard to ask because I don't think I deserve to know." He tipped his head back against the couch cushion. "I watch every single one of Cameron's milestones and I cherish them all, but at the back of my mind, there's a blank space where Shay's should be." He rubbed his hand over mine to take the sting of the words away. "And I feel so guilty. Especially when Shay's growing up. He's writing term papers for college and debating topics I barely under-stand, and now that he doesn't live here…"

"The disconnect deepens."

It took a second, but eventually, he nodded.

"I'm sorry, love."

His eyes immediately sought and caught mine. "Don't ever say sorry for raising our son and making him so damn smart and so damn *good*. I'm half-terrified that my influence on Cam will dumb him down! *Atomic* spiders." He groaned. "Jesus."

I snorted. "He's still a baby."

"My sperm's older. And that's my fault."

"Your fault, huh? Not sure you can help it. That's kind of how time works."

He wrinkled his nose. "You know what I mean."

"I do, and I also know that Cam will be Cam just like Shay's Shay. Maybe Cam will be smarter but won't give a fuck about saving the world. Maybe he'll be the next Blue Goblin—"

"Green," Declan corrected then huffed at my grin. "Look, you read enough of those damn stories and you pick up on some stuff."

"I never took you as a comic book kinda kid."

"Da thought they were for pussies."

That was no answer, but I closed my eyes. "I still want to strangle him. Frequently."

He crowed, "That's because you love me."

"I really do." I pressed my head against his shoulder and stared at the tree that taunted me with its emptiness. "I can't make up for the lost memories, and I know there are a million different things that I can't even remember, that were just life, that were a random Tuesday in a random March in a random year... but I can bring stuff up?"

"Like what?"

"Star started a curse jar for Kat. And Shay just brought up the one we had. Have to figure he inspired her... Wanna hear that story?"

The damn tree could wait.

His arms tightened around my waist as he sank us deeper into the cushions for our very own impromptu storytime. "You know I do."

FOUR

I SAW him from the back office.

At least, I saw the top of his head.

The spike in my hormones deduced the rest—I'd concluded a while back that some part of my hindbrain, that Neanderthal who prepared woolly mammoth for her caveman mate's breakfast, sprang to life whenever Finn neared me.

The notion had a smile dancing on my lips.

The only caveman-like aspect of Finn's nature was his attitude. Every other inch of him had the whole "city slicker" image down pat.

Which was ironic on all its own. My husband was a shark. Pure and simple.

I whistled under my breath. "What a way to go though…"

"Ugh, don't tell me. Finn just showed up?"

"Don't judge. Like you don't drool over Luc."

Jen, my BFF, studied her manicure. Somehow, she managed to maintain the sass over a video call. "He drools over me."

"It's a mutual drooling. Admit it." At her sniff, I pointed at her. "Aha! There. Right there. You were thinking of him and making doe eyes."

She rubbed her middle finger over her nose, but I only caught half of the show as more of Finn's head came into view.

"Ugh, I'm going. I refuse to watch you stalk and eye-fuck Finn long distance."

"Talk later?" I didn't even bother looking at her.

"After dinner. I still want to talk to you about..." She heaved a sigh. "Never mind. We'll discuss it when you're actually listening, bish."

I wafted a hand at her in farewell, confirmed that she'd ended the video call, then pushed my desk chair back and strode over to the wall of windows.

Unashamedly doing exactly what Jen had said—I stalked my DH through the two-way mirror setup that let me watch over both the shop floor and the bakery out back.

His movements were relaxed. Easy. A hand tucked into his pants pocket as he joked with Freddy, one of my apprentices who had a natural gift with sourdough starters. The gleam of his watch peeped at me, but it wasn't ostentatious. Just matter-of-fact.

He rarely left the city but had crossed into Jersey for a meeting today. Clearly, it had annoyed him—his hair was more rumpled than usual and he'd worked the knot of his tie loose.

I bit my lip as Betty, one of my newer employees, handed him an iced tea. Betty, uncaring that Finn owned parts of Manhattan and could bankrupt billionaires for shits and giggles, patted his cheek. Finn just blinked at her but accepted the iced tea and made a swift retreat.

I snorted when Betty lowered her head to check out his ass, then pursed her lips before shaking it off.

I called it "The Finn Effect."

Or maybe it was just Aidan Sr.'s genes—God knew, all his sons had inherited that "wow" factor.

Certifiable the man might have been, but he was undeniably more handsome than the devil.

When a soft tap sounded at my door, I didn't bother moving, just called over my shoulder, "Come in."

He arched a brow when he saw me standing by the windows. "You spying?"

"On Betty checking out your ass? What's the problem? That she's staring seventy-five in the face or that she pats your cheek like you're a toddler?"

"She gave me iced tea."

"On my orders."

He gaped at me. "What the hell?!"

"I knew you were coming to collect me and didn't want coffee breath to spoil my 'hello' kiss."

"Ohhh. Why didn't you just say so? That's what gum is for, wife," Finn growled, depositing the iced tea with a glower on a coaster on my desk—yes, it had taken the entire length of our marriage to train him to do that—and striding over to me.

I let him sweep me up in his arms with a happy sigh. My own slid along his shoulders, my wrists crossing at the back of his neck.

A warm glint appeared in his eyes. "Where's Jake?"

"With Star. I said we'd collect him on the way home."

He hummed. "This dress is new."

"Mayyyybe."

"No maybe about it." He pulled back a little so he could stare at it. "Ohh, it was tea with the coven today, wasn't it?"

"We're not witches."

"I never said you were. But they definitely are." He clucked his tongue. "Let me guess, Star's set fire to something and wanted Savannah to convince Aidan to let her get away with it?"

"Don't be mean."

"I'm being realistic. Or do I mean pragmatic? Or, hell, *optimistic?*"

"You mean all three." I released a soft laugh at his knowing look.

"Star hasn't set fire to anything as far as I'm aware. Though, Savannah was in a mood."

"Ahh. That'd explain why Aidan blew a fuse, huh?"

"Your meeting was with him?"

He just shrugged.

Enough said...

"She slept in the guest bedroom."

His brows shot up so high they almost touched his hairline. "Jesus Christ."

"Yep. He never mentioned it?"

"Not really. He was grouchier than usual. It led to him and Brennan getting into a fistfight."

"Wow."

"They've been bitching at each other for weeks. Mostly, I was glad for them to get it out of their system."

"Who won?"

"Who do you think? Brennan's gained eighty pounds in muscle since Aidan's started dumping more onto him. Bren's working out as stress relief." He hugged me to him, like I already wasn't close enough. "So, what happened between Aidan and Savannah?"

"She said she asked him some questions about animal fighting within the city limits and he refused to answer."

Finn frowned. "I haven't heard anything about any animal fights."

"You're the money man," I said lightly, stroking the whorls of hair at his nape. "Why would you know?"

"Fair point. She should have asked Brennan. Aidan takes a step back on a lot of that shit now."

"Ahh, yes, while you guys plan world domination."

"Don't mock. It'll work. One day."

I rolled my eyes but leaned up on tiptoe, grateful when he lowered his head to kiss me.

"That's better. Why didn't we do that immediately?"

"You wanted to bicker about iced tea."

"I'm a fucking idiot."

Humming in agreement, I brushed my lips over his, sighing happily when his hand settled on my ass. His knuckles began toying with the velvet fabric, rubbing back and forth as he grabbed my pillowy softness.

Was I surprised when he turned us around so that he was pressed against the two-way window and I faced the office? Nope. Finn's fascination with my butt ran as deep as my own with his.

Betty's too, probably.

A wild spark fluttered through me—possessiveness. He was mine. Nobody else's. The trials and tribulations of our married life had proven that if nothing else.

Finn was undeniably, categorically *mine*.

A happy sound escaped me when his other hand tugged up my skirt until the hem tickled the backs of my thighs. His teeth snagged my bottom lip, and after a quick bite, he rumbled, "Here or the desk?"

"Desk." I moaned as he nipped my ear. "Please."

He lifted me in that way of his, like I weighed nothing more than a feather, and it never failed to enchant me.

Or make me crave getting into his pants.

When he perched me on the edge, I ruched up my skirt until it sat at the tops of my thighs and leaned back against the blotter. My computer hummed beside me, and the iced tea he'd brought along was a sticky threat to the sanctity of my workspace, but I so didn't give a shit.

Expectation fluttered through me when he dropped to his knees with a smirk and yanked my thighs forward so that he could better situate my feet. One, he propped on his shoulders, the other on the guest chair in front of my desk.

When he smoothed my skirt higher, a guttural groan escaped him. "You were walking around the city with no underwear on?"

"What can I say? I'm a planner."

He rested his head on my leg, scant inches away from my core.

Finn had scorched any body shame out of my being after Jake's birth, so I had no problem with his proximity to my pussy.

Aside from the fact that he was more bothered about looking at it than touching it…

I tipped my hips upward. "If you don't want to sleep in the guest bedroom too—"

Yelping when he nipped the softness of my inner thigh, I laughed when he growled. "No guest bed for me."

"Or me?"

"Never." His arms clutched at my hips, the claim of ownership sending shivers down my spine. "I can see how wet you are for me, baby. Been thinking about this?"

"Knew you were coming to pick me up," I agreed, aware I sounded breathless. "We haven't baptized my office in a while."

He clucked his tongue. "An oversight on my part."

His nose nuzzled along the soft expanse of my thigh until I could feel his breath brushing my pussy lips. I jerked in surprise when he blew a stream over my clit.

One of my hands fell into the artlessly tousled waves atop his head, and I groaned as, finally, he made direct contact.

His tongue fluttered over the small nub before that stream of air sent more shivers rushing down my spine. The warmth combined with the chill had the muscles in my legs tensing and relaxing.

When he began to nibble and play with my folds, I let my nails burrow into his scalp. Long, teasing licks toyed with the entirety of my sex, reminding me that Finn had never misunderstood how the clitoris worked. Everything down below was his for exploration, and it always made me feel so *seen*.

Finn savored me.

Because *I* was his favorite treat.

My heel dug into his shoulder when he ran the tip around my slit then hissed as he thrust his tongue inside me a few times while his thumb caressed the nub—so tenderly that my toes curled.

"Finn," I moaned. "Don't tease. I've waited the whole day for this."

"The whole day, huh?" The words vibrated over my sensitized core.

I stared at him, experiencing a sharp thrill when I saw how my juices coated his lips and mouth, even parts of his jaw.

"Yes. Been dreaming about this since I woke up."

He pressed an open kiss to my clit. "You dreamed about me going down on you?"

When he wiggled his tongue from side to side, I rasped, "More like you fucking me."

His brow arched as he suckled.

"Oh, God—"

That earned me a wicked smile. "Not God. Just your husband."

"Yesss. *My* husband."

His lips curved, which felt so good around the bundle of nerves, especially when he tested it with his teeth. Not hard enough to sting, just a careful warning that had me cascading into mush.

On the verge of overstimulation, I gawked blindly at my office ceiling, completely uncaring about how he'd splayed me on my desk, that anyone could knock on the door at any minute—all that mattered boiled down to his mouth, my pussy, and the incoming orgasm.

My eyes fluttered shut as he continued devouring me, supping from me like I was a meal and he hadn't eaten in days. Every inch of my cunt earned his attention like time didn't matter to him, and his fingers went to work, thrusting into me, spreading me wide.

"Finn." My foot arched, toes digging into his shoulder this time. "Oh god, baby, I'm going to come. Please. Don't stop. Fuck. No. Right —" I pressed my hand to my mouth and bit down on the fleshiest part as he took me straight through one orgasm and had me approaching the precipice of another.

I hovered there, dangling at his mercy as every single nerve ending went to war inside me. His tongue, teeth, and lips were soldiers in a fight I could never win.

When he jerked to his feet, I stared at him in bewilderment, going so far as to hunch up on my elbows, but seeing him free his cock from his pants had me jerking upright to help him.

When the iced tea wiggled precariously, he moved it, *sans* coaster—it barely made it onto my register.

Instead, I unfastened his zipper while he worked on his belt. As I drew him out, that thick, branding heat already scoring me, I saw pre-cum grace my palm.

Letting go of his cock, I lifted my hand, tilted it just so, and moved my tongue over the creases in the skin there. Running it along the tiny folds as I scooped him up.

His eyes, mesmerized and glued to my mouth, burned.

His hands kneaded the fleshier parts of my outer thighs as he watched me torment him, then he bowed his head and tracked my movements so our tongues twined against my palm. While I'd cleaned it of his seed, I could taste my juices on him—literal proof of my release.

The rawness of that union, wet and dirty and pure *us* had me mewling as his hips burrowed between my legs, and I braced myself for impact.

Sparks of electricity cascaded inside me as he tapped his dick against my softness. I already knew I was wet, but the sounds were close to obscene as he rubbed his cock all over my folds. Marking me with his pre-cum but also triggering every erogenous zone on his personal must-visit list.

All the while, his tongue tangled with mine, until finally the tip of his shaft found my slit.

I hissed then groaned when, slowly, well aware of how sensitive I was after an orgasm, he thrust into me.

My pussy clutched at him. Even after so many years together, an inherent sense of panic at how big he was stole my breath. Then, he yanked on my hip, which tipped my pelvis up and he sank in the whole way.

Pressing me into the desk, he shoved my keyboard aside so office furniture couldn't attack me and tugged on the neckline of my dress. My tits spilled free, framed by a festive emerald velvet, and he groaned at the sight.

When he bit my nipple, I dragged my nails through his hair and yanked him away from the sensitive bud.

He pinned his elbows next to my ears then and dived onto me— lips reuniting, tongues entwining. Noisy and wet and so fucking perfect.

We were in my bakery. My staff worked out front. A glass of iced tea remained in serious peril, and my velvet dress would be the direct target. But at that moment, all I saw was him. All I cared about was *this*. Us. All that mattered was he didn't stop. That he never stopped.

I kicked up my legs to hold him close, crossing them at the ankles because I couldn't have borne for him to leave me. The edge of the desk dug into the softness of my ass, but I simply didn't give a shit.

I needed this. Him. More. More. More.

With our lips locked together, there was no room for words, no breath for talking. Just kissing. Just reuniting. Just colliding.

I ran my hands through his hair again, loving how he groaned into the kiss. I loved it even more when it encouraged him to speed up.

Slow but deep thrusts turned into rapid-fire ones that I'd feel in my core later, but I didn't mind. I enjoyed the reminder. I loved how that faint memory lingered... It always made me crave more.

I writhed underneath him because he kept us so closely bound, barely pulling out of me before he was back inside, that the pressure on my sex remained constant.

It wasn't like direct stimulation, but it had me keening through an orgasm as he pumped his hips until he groaned, "Fuuuuck," into my mouth.

I swallowed it and never let the kiss stop. I guessed I should say that the kiss kept us quiet, but it had nothing to do with volume and propriety and just me never wanting his mouth to break away from mine.

I wanted his air. His breath.

It belonged to me.

Just like he'd vowed all those years ago...

Eventually, he slumped on top of me. I felt the sudden exhaustion in his body, the sagging of his muscles, the fading of that ever-present inner tension that brimmed inside him like the predator he was. And I reveled in it.

He rarely lost control, and never failed to be careful with me, but today, he'd forgotten that he'd used my desk to fuck me.

As my heartbeat calmed and his breathing returned to normal, I stroked my fingers through his hair again. I always savored the closeness. These moments of silence. Stillness. It built the most rugged of bonds, reinforcing them over and over until they were unbreakable.

"I should head into Jersey more often, huh?"

That those were his first words had me chuckling, especially because he slurred them. "It wasn't exactly Timbuktu."

I saw his smug smile from the side, where his nose nestled into my breast, and rolled my eyes. "You missed me."

My fingertips trickled over his brow and his eyelids, where faint lines had begun to take hold. They danced onto his jaw and slid along his lips. "I always miss you." When he made to speak, I pushed a digit between them. "Don't spoil my post-orgasm glow by bragging."

I snickered at the glint in his eye but kept my fingers in his mouth, mostly because Finn's oral fetish would never fail to fascinate me, especially when he sucked on them.

The sharp buzz of pleasure sang through my veins. I thrust them deeper then—

A knock sounded at the door.

"Fuck."

His tongue prodded between my fingers.

My toes curled again, but I pulled them free with a hiss as he gifted the pads with two sharp nips.

"Just a second," I hollered, but I was pouting.

When he straightened up and tucked his dick away, I huffed.

Then huffed some more as he gently lifted the neckline of my dress and helped me sit up once he'd put me to rights.

As the aches from the hard surface made themselves known to me, I grouched, "Why did I want to do this on my desk again?"

Crazier still, why was I beyond ready for round two?!

"Memories?" he teased.

"Oh, yeah. I'll be happy about it tomorrow." As I jumped down, already feeling the quickening loss of him inside me, I yelped when I took some of the blotter with me. The iced tea, safe throughout our endeavors, tumbled over.

Finn managed to snag the glass before the entire contents upended over my desk, laughing all the while. My nose scrunched as I dove for a paper towel from the bathroom. More bothered about cleaning up the mess than myself.

Walking around with Finn inside me was never a hardship...

While I blotted the excess liquid, he joked, "Iced tea is *always* a bad idea."

"Definitely chew gum next time," I grumbled. Then, a random thought hit. "We need to take Jake to see Santa. Aela told me she took Cameron earlier this morning."

"It's in my calendar."

"Did you put it in mine?"

"For the day itself and with two reminders prior."

"Huh. You're pretty good at this parenting shit, aren't you?"

With a wink, Finn pressed a kiss to the fingertips he'd just nibbled on. "I had a good teacher."

FIVE

"MOTHERFUCKER—"

I popped my head out of the living room and, eyes wide, discovered Brennan and Aidan squaring up outside the pool room.

"I told you to back the fuck off."

"You're the one who won't goddamn listen. You give me this role that I never asked for, when I was doing most of the fucking work anyway, and now you have the audacity to—"

"Brennan?" I uttered his name softly, so as not to surprise either of them.

Just one look and I could tell they'd already been fighting and were on the brink of a rematch. Disheveled clothing aside, they sported various cuts and nicks. From here, I saw how raw each of their knuckles were.

Both heads whipped around to find me, and I simply arched a brow at them.

Gone were the days when either of these men had the power to scare me.

My husband had done too good a job of teaching me how important I was to him.

"I think we need coffee," I declared when they both just looked at me. "And brownies. I stopped at Aoife's and picked up some treats. Come into the kitchen." When they frowned, I narrowed my eyes. "Now."

Brennan's nostrils flared, but Aidan shook his shoulders, released a breath, and growled, "Fine."

I nodded as he strode toward me then beckoned my hand at Brennan. His jaw worked but he traipsed after his brother, only pausing along the way to brush a kiss to my temple.

"You're not supposed to get involved when we fight."

"I'm not letting either of you ruin my buzz."

"Your buzz?" He tangled our fingers together. "Afternoon tea amped up a notch?"

"Oh yeah, we had strippers and everything—" I chortled when he scowled. "I'm joking, Brennan. *Joking*." At his grunt, I ghosted my fingertips over a graze on his cheek. "You fought?"

His lips pursed. "You said you had brownies?"

I nodded and watched him trundle off to the kitchen.

Aidan leaned against the counter, his fingers already in the box of baked goods I'd just purchased. Brennan, of course, snatched the muffin he was about to eat and, out of spite, took a massive bite.

"Brennan, you don't even like blueberry muffins," I chided.

"I took it in your honor. They're your favorites."

"My hero," I sniped. "Now, do I have to invite your mother over, or shall I just bang your heads together without her input?"

Aidan snagged a donut. "Ma's at the spa."

"You're a poet and you don't fucking know it."

"Brennan." When that earned me his version of a pout, I sighed. "What's going on? Savannah was really upset today, Aidan. I hope you know you're pissing people off left, right, and center."

"She asks too many questions."

"Duh. Marriage hasn't exactly mellowed her out, has it?"

"It definitely fucking hasn't," he griped then took an extra-large bite of his donut.

As much as the sweet treats stopped them from arguing, it also meant their mouths were too busy to answer my questions.

"Well?" I tapped my toe on the Italian marble that Brennan had imported especially because I loved the color.

"You're not my wife, Camille. I don't have to—"

"Watch your fucking tone," Brennan snapped. "Don't you dare talk to her like that in HER home."

"Like what? A human? It's your job to lick her ass, not mine."

My eyes widened when both of them dove at each other. "Not my—" My shoulders sagged. "—*table*." The damn thing, six feet long and over 200 pounds of raw mahogany that had needed assembling *in situ*, nearly flew across the floor as they fell into it.

When they veered toward the dresser that displayed my collection of Delft miniature houses, I squeaked and darted into the pantry.

I had no idea what made me do it.

Maybe it was invoking the threat of Lena? (She gave off poltergeist vibes.)

Grateful I'd been weight training with Brennan recently, I picked up the copper holder that I stored my potatoes in, hugged it to my chest, and ran back into the kitchen.

In the time I'd been gone, they'd angled away from the dresser, but seeing as they rolled around the floor like maniacs, only God knew how long my miniatures would be safe.

I got as close as I dared, lifted the copper urn, then upended it.

Right over them.

More than twenty pounds of potatoes cascaded over their heads, dirt and little wiggly roots that had fallen loose alongside them.

"What the fuck?!" Aidan roared, spluttering as he choked on potato dust, ducking left and right to avoid the fallout.

"Jesus Christ," Brennan snarled, whipping around to evade the projectiles, but gravity wouldn't be stopped.

Even as the brothers rolled out of the way, they landed on the potatoes.

Now that my container was empty, I ignored their yelps and barked, "Have you two quite finished?! Roman is taking a goddamn nap, and if you woke him up, I'll hurl my crisper at you!"

They both stared up at me, filthy in the most literal ways, potatoes on their chests and between their legs, pooling around their shoulders. Smudges on their faces, dust in their expensive suits. Dirt in their hair and spattered around them like a farmer had outlined their bodies instead of the police with chalk.

When they continued staring at me, I stacked my hands on my hips. "You do not fight in my kitchen. Do you know how long it took me to find a damn table I liked? And my miniatures!"

Aidan and Brennan ceased gawking at me to glance at one another and, as if the fight were a fever dream, began to roar with laughter.

Aidan slapped Brennan's chest in time to his wheezing chuckles, and my husband, well, he *guffawed*.

I didn't even know Brennan could make that noise.

It was my turn to gape at them as they laughed themselves hoarse. I'd never seen two of the city's most brutal men look this damn young.

"*Blyad*," I muttered when it carried on and on. I even ended up plunking myself onto one of the chairs that had screeched across the floor during their fight.

Eventually, the pair of them gasped for breath but stopped with the hyena act.

"You married Ma," Aidan joked. "All she needed was a rolling pin—"

"I know," Brennan wheezed.

"I am here?"

Aidan's head tipped backward to find me. "Sorry, Camille."

I sniffed. "I'd accept your apology if my kitchen weren't a damn mess."

Aidan punched Brennan's arm—but in a friendly way. God help me for knowing the difference. These damn brothers were going to turn me gray! "Come on, let's clear this up before she brings out the rolling pin for real."

Brennan, like the frickin' ninja he was, did this weird jump/leap and landed on his feet. For a big man, the stunts he could pull always boggled my mind. Either he *was* a part-time ninja or just part cat.

Brennan yanked Aidan to his feet, taunting, "Come on, old man."

Aidan flipped him the bird, but they both surprised me...

Neither of these men had so much as lifted a broom or a mop in decades. I wasn't even sure Brennan knew we had them, but he proved me wrong.

Within minutes, the pair of them were sweeping up the mess they'd made.

"Remember the last time we did this?" Aidan asked with a laugh.

"When Da threw a fucking fit about Eoghan enlisting," Brennan said wryly. To me, he clarified, "Eoghan was supposed to be one of us."

"I thought Sr. was proud of him?"

"Oh, he was. Eventually. And he definitely appreciated the skills Eoghan picked up on Uncle Sam's dime, but first, he threw Eoghan into Ma's dresser." Brennan shot me an apologetic look. "I'm glad we didn't bust any of your miniatures, honey. I'm sorry about the mess."

"Apology only accepted if you promise not to fight in my damn home again."

He raised his hands in surrender, broom included. "Promise."

"What did Lena collect?"

Aidan's gaze turned distant. "Those ugly as fuck flower things."

"Oh, shit, yeah, I forgot about them. *Capi do manti?*"

"*Capodimante?*" I corrected.

"That's right. Porcelain stuff."

My brow puckered. "How sad for her!"

"Yeah. Da was an asshole. That temper of his—" Brennan and Aidan shared a look when he broke off.

Simultaneously, they cleared their throats.

"Sorry, Camille."

"Sorry, baby."

I laughed at their puppy-dog expressions. "Three apologies are enough, and you're not your father."

Aidan scrubbed the back of his neck. "Hard to remember that sometimes."

"It bothers each of you that you might be emulating him," I reasoned, knowing that for all they loved their father, his specter would haunt them for the rest of their lives. "But unlike you, he didn't give a damn about being his *raw* self."

"Ain't that the truth," Brennan complained.

"At least you know what to buy your mother for Christmas."

They stared at me in confusion.

"Jeez, men can be real slow sometimes. The porcelain figures!"

"Nah, she doesn't like that stuff anymore."

"How do you know, Aidan?"

"Well, have you ever seen any in her apartment?"

"No, but maybe that's because she misses her old collection. It'll be different if you guys find her some pieces. It'll mean more to her."

Brennan rubbed his chin. "You think she'd like that?"

"I think there's no harm in trying, *and* I know she's going on a cruise, so if she hates them, you won't get a vat of mashed potatoes hurled at you over the dinner table."

Both men laughed, but from the glance they shot one another, the second in as many minutes, I figured they knew I wasn't wrong.

Lena might be getting older, and that red hair of hers might be more silver now, but the fire in her could burn the bravest of souls.

While they worked on sweeping up their mess, I made us coffee. With that prepared, I set it on the newly straightened table and chairs, then plopped the rest of the treats on top.

"Now, what were you two bickering about?" At my pointed looks, they also took their seats.

"Business, sweetheart—"

"Don't 'sweetheart' me, Brennan O'Donnelly."

He grunted.

"Savannah slept in the guest bedroom."

Aidan's announcement had my husband frowning, but I just nodded. "She said as much."

My brother-in-law winced. "She told you guys?"

"They share every-fucking-thing," Brennan mumbled. "I told you."

Aidan cringed. "She still mad?"

"Hurt, more like."

"Damn." He dragged a hand through his hair then grimaced when he tracked dirt alongside it. "I don't understand why she can't leave some shit alone."

"You knew what she was like from the beginning."

"Some bull is easier to discuss than others."

"She said something about animal fighting?"

"Fuck's sake!"

"They share everything." Brennan took a bite of a brownie when I frowned at him.

"You hurt her, Aidan."

"I didn't mean to."

I arched a brow. "That doesn't make it better."

His gaze dropped to the table. "Some shit, I don't want to share with her. Some shit, I want to spare her from. This fucking city is riddled with corruption and horrible, horrible crap. Is it too much to want to come home and just be with her? Not have her pepper me with goddamn questions about things that'll screw with her head?"

"Mostly, he was pissed she knew something he didn't," Brennan taunted.

"Fuck you!"

"Have you talked to her about this?" I interrupted with a glare at the pair of them.

"No."

"Then how is she supposed to know how you feel?"

He harrumphed.

"You might think you're protecting her. You might even think that you just want her to be your safe space, Aidan. But if you don't tell her, she can never get with the program." While he blinked at me, I continued, "And what happened between you two?"

"We couldn't pinpoint a location where Savannah said the illegal fights are happening," Brennan drawled.

"So there is a place in the tristate area holding those kinds of… events?"

"Hmm."

I rolled my eyes at the nonanswer. "You were trying to shut them down?"

"Of course. That shit's fucking obscene. I'll watch two men fight to the death because they *chose* to be so goddamn dumb. Two dogs didn't have a choice," Aidan snapped. "Savannah told me this was happening. My wife. And she cried, Camille. She was in tears. Her massive heart was breaking and I couldn't fucking—"

When he broke off and sucked in a sharp breath, I patted his shoulder. "Aidan?"

"What?"

"You were coming from a good place, but you communicated that to her poorly. She was already sad about the brutal reality of life in NYC and you made that worse. Things like this hit differently when you're a mom. Knowing the world you brought a child into is rotten to the core makes you bear the weight of it like it's your own sin." *Boy, did I feel that burden every day.* "You need to apologize to her, tell her that you're trying to make it right and that you only got angry because you want to protect her and Third. Take chocolates too—she was well into the desserts by the time we left."

"That's it?"

I shrugged. "Be sincere."

"I've never been in the doghouse with her before. Not really." He scratched his chin. "We always just jump straight to the make-up sex."

"As Star told her, that's because she thinks with her clitoris." At his smirk, I tutted. "The clitoris is disengaged. Don't be a jerk. Just be kind. And apologize.

"If you pick a fight with my husband tomorrow because you had to spend another night alone and because you guys can't find an illegal fight in a haystack, then potatoes are the least of your worries."

His grin was sharper than a blade. "I have my orders, huh?"

Brennan smirked. "She comes by it honestly."

Aidan rapped his knuckles on the table then got to his feet. "Can I blame you if it doesn't work?"

"Of course it'll work."

Aidan dipped down to kiss my cheek. "Thanks for the advice."

I nodded. "See you later."

"Yup. Bye, fucker."

"Bye, shitface."

Their farewells had me huffing, but not before I squealed as Brennan yanked me onto his lap through some feat that defied the laws of physics.

He cupped my cheeks. "Was it hard?"

"Was what hard?"

"When you fell from heaven, baby."

Though I burst out laughing, I gently brushed my fingers over one of the newer bruises on his throat of all places. "You crackpot."

"Your crackpot."

"Agreed. Aidan's lucky I fed him and didn't poison him." At his arched brow, I groused, "You have more bruises than him."

"What have we learned in the gym?"

"You can bend me over the treadmill as easily as you can bend me over the bed?"

He shot me a cocky smile. "What else?"

"Ahhh, you mean his damage is below the collar?"

"If he isn't pissing blood all week, then my name's not Brennan O'Donnelly."

"So, what you're telling me is that I'm going to get a call from Savannah when she realizes she can bounce on her husband's dick again and it's not fully functioning?"

"Hey, it'll function. It's his kidneys I rearranged. You don't need kidneys to fuck."

"Every science teacher in the country just groaned."

"Then I did them proud."

My lips quirked as I settled into the snug fit of his lap and the nook between him and the table. "You okay? I heard some of what you said."

"He drives me crazy." His gaze shifted to stare over the expanse of the city behind me. "No change there. I'll be screaming into the void about this for fucking years. Don't worry about it."

"I do though." I sighed and rested my head between his throat and shoulder, where it scented of bergamot and orange. Which meant he kinda smelled like my favorite Earl Grey, and that was *not* a complaint. Knowing him, it was intentional too. "I always worry about you, Brennan. I love you."

He managed to press another kiss to my forehead. "I love you too, Camille."

"I'm here, you know?"

"I know, but for once, I get where Aidan's coming from. It's so fucking shit out there, Camille, and sparing you from that feels like my goddamn husbandly duty." His shoulders slumped. "Like, it's never been good, but somehow it's getting worse. There's no honor anymore—"

"There never was!" I hooted. "Animal baiting is hardly new, love. Disgusting, yes, but not new. My father used to have a place he went to in Russia because the ones here tended to be raided. It's horrific. That you and the rest of your brothers have standards makes you infinitely better than the men who ruled before you."

"Don't make out like we're the good guys, babe," he said dryly.

"Oh, I'm well aware of the many and varied ways you all do vile shit, but..." I hitched a shoulder. "...you have to understand. My father was an abusive asshole who tormented my mother into an early grave. He broke her systemically, until she was nothing more than something for him to toy with. Inessa doesn't remember half the horrors he put our mother through.

"Your da loved Lena but his world still broke her.

"Just by giving a damn about your family, by having wives you love and who you shelter from your business, kids you protect and value as more than future heirs, means you'll make a change."

"You're an idealist, and you're painting us with halos we don't deserve. But... thank you."

I didn't know how long we sat there. I just knew that his arms remained fixed around me for a long time.

For me, forever wouldn't be enough.

I told him as much, and his laughter was as gruff as his earlier words, so I chided, "You're doing something right."

He sighed. "As long as you think so, baby. You're the only one who matters."

And I felt that in my soul.

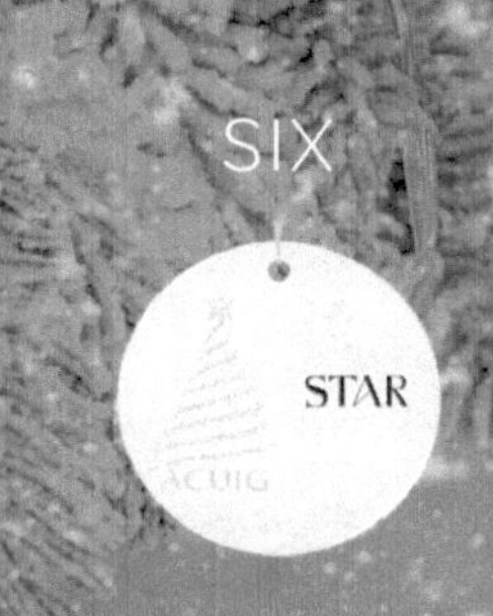

SIX

"WHO ARE WE KILLING?"

I stacked the Magni-Focuser on top of my head so I could stare at him, ignoring the fact that only Beavis was by his side and the other Shih Tzu wasn't—

There.

I jumped as he sniffed my feet and tried to lick them.

"No one's dying today. Unless it's this damn dog. Why is Butthead so obsessed with my feet?!"

"You have pretty feet and my dogs have great taste," Conor dismissed as he narrowed his eyes in suspicion.

"I don't need a supervisor," I grouched when he leaned on my desk to watch me work.

Then I proceeded to shriek once a tiny tongue went straight between my toes!

"Clearly, you do. You're making a bomb and—"

"I'm not making a bomb."

"We agreed—you're not allowed to kill people anymore."

"I thought I just wasn't allowed a gun."

"You and small print, Jesus Christ. No killing. I conceded to maiming and torture for that sex trafficker in Lima, but no. Killing."

"Luckily for our deal, I'm not reneging. This isn't a bomb."

"Sure it is."

"That tells me how many bombs *you* have built because I'm making crackers."

"Like what my ma drags out on the Christmas table on the 25th cracker...?"

"Well, I'm not talking about the ones you pair with cheese, Conor, sheesh."

"Not explosives?"

"No!" I scowled at his continued suspicion then leaned down to pick up Butthead and shoved the fluff ball at Conor. "I'm making Christmas crackers, dammit. Now, take your foot-fetishist of a dog and let me concentrate."

He tucked B-head under his arm. For lap dogs, Conor never let them sit on his lap. They were either his sentries *or* he lugged them around like a football. "Why?"

"Because."

"That's no answer."

"Secret Santa."

He pinched the bridge of his nose. "Is this 'let's just throw random ass words at Conor' day?"

"It can be if you'd like."

"You're still eating Halloween candy corn because of me and—"

"Don't make out like I didn't thank you."

"The least you could do is clue me in! Who's the Secret Santa with? Troy and Cin?!"

"Actually, your sisters-in-law. Because if you think Troy and Cin are afraid to exchange guns with me for Secret Santa, you're mistaken."

He ignored that. "They're your in-laws too."

"I'm not claiming them officially. You have no choice."

"You're not claiming them but you're making them a fucking cracker?"

"Not them. One of them. Jesus, you really don't know how Secret Santa works, huh?"

He gusted out his cheeks. "I thought Santa *was* secret."

"Tell me you're rich…"

"Like you're not too."

"Well, I used to do Secret Santa with my dad's roadies."

"Explain."

"What a roadie is?" I taunted.

He flipped me the bird.

"Secret Santa is where you put everyone's name in a bag, and then you pick someone and you keep it a secret who you're gifting something to."

"Why wasn't I involved?"

"Were you at today's afternoon tea?"

"Well, no—"

"Then how could you be involved?"

"That's not fair!"

"If you want to hear about Declan pissing in front of Aela—"

"YOU TALK ABOUT THAT?!"

I smirked. "We talk about all kinds of stuff."

"No way."

"Yes way."

"Nothing's sacred?!" he sputtered in horror.

"Nope."

"This sounds like a breach of my human rights."

"Be grateful you're not Aidan. We know more shit about his cock than I'm sure *he* does. Though, not today. Vana was pouting."

"Yeah, he's been in a crappy mood all day too."

"Anything I can help with?"

"Nah. I'm working on it." He peered at my handiwork. "You sure that's not a bomb?"

"I'm fucking sure. Jesus, Conor." I flipped down my loops. "Fuck off if you're going to ask irritating questions."

"So... you're making the popper?"

"Yes."

"Can't you just buy that stuff?"

"Where'd be the fun in that? Potassium nitrate—"

"Gunpowder?!"

"Yep." I pointed to the strips I was carefully dousing in my solution. "These detonate the explosive when you pull them apart and the rapid combustion makes the pop."

"Sounds like a bomb to me."

"It's a miniature explosion. Don't exaggerate."

His lips pursed. "If you're making these, then they won't be so mini. I know you. You wouldn't make them if you weren't hoping for a *bang*."

"You're half-right. I do want a bang, but I'm not going to have anyone lose their hands. Well, unless Aidan keeps on pissing off Savannah..."

"This sounds like a lot of work."

"Nah. I like it. Good times—reminds me of chemistry and my boner for Mr. Wensley."

"Nerd."

"You can't judge."

"True."

"Who was your teacher crush?"

"I had a couple. Madame Ducharme was my favorite French teacher—"

"You had a native speaker?"

"French Canadian. Know what the French Canadians call a blueberry?"

"Nope."

"A *bleuet*."

I cackled. "Why is that funny?"

"Probably because it sounds like the cartoon dog." Grinning, Conor got to his feet. "You sure I can't help?"

"Nope."

"Who'd you pick for Secret Santa? Savannah?"

"That'd be telling. But warn Aidan that I'll make sure he gets one of my creations if he doesn't make it up to my sister from another mister."

"Duly noted," he said wryly before strolling over to his desk, depositing Butthead in the bed that Beavis had already fled to, then bribing them both with those stinky-ass dried bull cocks they adored.

"Everything okay with Jake?"

"Yup. Finn just came by to pick him up."

"Good. The others?"

"Niall's out for the count."

"Figured as much. Hasn't uttered a peep on the security system. One advantage to him, Roman, and Third being the same age is they exhaust each other when they're together. Plus, putting up his tree was hell so that had to take away his wings. Benjamim's still with his English tutor, right?"

"Yup, and Kat's throwing imaginary daggers at a textbook."

"Goooood."

We'd expected to adopt a baby a couple Januaries back, but instead we'd been gifted a six-year-old Brazilian boy who we'd spared, within fucking days, from a child brothel in Rio.

I still shuddered to think about how close it had been. Conor, despite his dislike of planes, had flown in to get him across to the US, and we'd dealt with the paperwork afterward.

Two years in, my beautiful Benji spoke English perfectly and understood everything after being indoctrinated by Kat and LyLy, my cousin, in the ways of Cartoon Network, but he needed extra help for classes, as reading/writing were his weakest skills.

As I carefully applied my solution to the strip, I asked, "You the reason that Eoghan was watching us today when Inessa, Camille, Savvie, and I took the kids to Aoife's bakery?"

His head whipped around so fast, it was a wonder it didn't fall off. "What? Who? When?! Why?! I mean. No."

Not suspicious. At all.

"Hmm."

"I'm not!"

Inessa had only managed to sneak off because I'd seen his scope and fucked with his visibility.

I had no idea where my sister-in-law went, nor was it any of my business, but fuck if I'd let Eoghan get away with being a creep.

"Is he still blackmailing you about your ma's stuffing?" At his silence, I drawled, "Because I can make him regret the day your da gave Lena—"

"Don't even finish that sentence." Conor scowled. "And he isn't blackmailing me."

"You're surveilling her for him, aren't you?"

"Hardly."

"Liar."

"It isn't surveillance. Not when you can do the same on your phone."

I hummed. "If you say so."

Fucking dipshits.

With the kiddos occupied/asleep, and without Conor and the gruesome twosome distracting me, I worked steadily through the strips I was creating.

My signature blend had been a party favor when my dad had toured. Just enough bang to make your ears pop but with a twist.

The techies had ended up adapting it and using it in the shows. Controlled explosions, FTW.

Whistling under my breath once I finished an hour later, I pushed them to the side and checked a couple of my programs. None of them were showing any results as of yet, and while I was virtually stalking two people in Riga, one in Johannesburg, and another in Helsinki, I figured they were in bed because of the time difference.

Stretching my shoulders, I twisted my hips a little then got to my feet. It was my turn to stroll over to Conor's desk and check out his current project.

Thankfully, both hellhounds were snoring and chasing imaginary rabbits in dreamland.

As I scanned through his directives, my brows lifted.

"What the fuck are you looking for?"

"Someplace big enough to host fights."

"Is Acuig diversifying and you just never told me?"

"Nah. Savannah heard a rumor, and Aidan wants me to check it out. So far, it's looking like it's hearsay." He twisted his chair around and encouraged me to sit on his lap. "Kat got detention yesterday. Did she tell you?"

I looped my arms around his neck. "Little shit. No, she didn't. She's been pumping me for cash all day too."

"Don't hate the player, hate the game."

"I could strangle you for teaching her that saying."

He chuckled. "It's true though."

I just sniffed. "What did she get detention for?"

"Misbehaving in class."

"The lessons aren't stimulating her." I pulled a face. "Not just a little shit, but a clever one."

"Too clever. For her own good. Think we need to discuss her moving up a grade?"

"She already has and she isn't settling in well. You know she hates most of the kids in her class."

"I don't blame her. They're horrible little fuckers. We can tutor her—"

"No. I told you. No homeschooling! She needs some normalcy and neither of us are that. I work in my PJs, you don't sleep when you're in the middle of a project, and we're the literal poster children for people with zero work/life balance."

"Maybe additional tutors then."

"She already has four!"

"More won't hurt. She's understimulated."

I wiggled my head. "That's an idea, I guess, but you watch her prioritize the subjects she's interested in."

"Of course." He dropped a kiss on my lips. "I hated school. It never stimulated me, and I struggled to find a baseline that worked. If we can help her, I want to."

"Be a mom, they said. Best job in the world, they said. No one told me I'd have to make decisions like an adult!"

"You've been rocking those decisions, babe. You didn't know your kid was gonna be a genius. Just be grateful we are and that we know what she's going through."

"I swear she has an old head on young shoulders." I huffed. "Fine, we'll talk to her about getting more tutors in subjects that'll extend her reach, like in Mandarin or something, but only if she keeps up her grades at school."

"That's the priority," he agreed. "We don't want her falling behind."

"What was she doing when you grabbed us some coffee? I left her with homework."

"Cartwheels, mostly."

"Damn. She only does those now when she's procrastinating or when Jake and Cam beg her to do a routine in the living room." I blinked. "You ever think she's growing up really fast?"

"I think all kids grow up faster than their parents are comfortable with."

"Stop being reasonable."

"What can I say? It's in my DNA."

"Oh, yeah. *Sure.*"

"She *has* finished procrastinating. She'd almost completed her homework."

"That's a relief. I told her we'd head to the pool after we put her and Benji's tree up. You coming?"

"To see you in your swimsuit? Hell, yeah, I'm coming."

My lips twitched. "Only you'd think my one-piece was hot."

"Hey, *Baywatch* was my jam."

"Want me to run in slow motion?"

"I mean… if the kids decide they prefer to watch TV? Sure. Treat me."

I tapped his chin. "You'll get a treat if you find me a STEM tutor. Maybe if she can design a bridge in her spare time, it'll stop her being bored. I fucking hate that word now. I actually feel sorry for my dad, and that's just obscene."

"Consider it done." Hands on my ass, he stood up with me in his arms, smirking all the while.

Because this wasn't the first time I'd let him lug me around, I rested my chin on his shoulder as he carried me into the living room, where Christmas had officially vomited over the apartment.

I'd never really thought about how awesome it'd be to have a partner. One who shared the burden and who I could trust to do the job right—but that's what Conor had become for me.

I knew that if I gave him a task, he'd follow through with it. Give him parameters and my man was a boss at checking off items on his to-do list.

Was there anything hotter?

I kissed his throat, just because.

Then kissed him again because he'd helped me decorate all six of our Christmas trees without a single complaint.

His low chuckle made my lips tingle.

"Can we have a 'no kiss' jar too?"

"If you want me to be poor, sure," Conor reasoned as my precocious brat popped up, armed with her version of Cerberus—Crepe and Suzette. AKA Ren and Stimpy.

"*I'd* be rich."

"I'm a hacker, Kat. Who do you think would end up with the dough?" I mocked.

"That's stealing!"

Her gasp had me cackling. "What is it you think we do, Kat?"

Her stumped expression lit me up like a firework.

Honestly, my kid never shut the fuck up and here she was, sputtering for words.

"Is that... silence? It's been so long since I heard it," Conor joked.

My cackling morphed into outright laughter, and when he put me down on the back of the couch, I held my stomach because it hurt so bad.

"Don't be mean!" Kat pouted, peering around Conor's arm to glower at me.

Her fingers weren't so tiny anymore, not like they used to be, but they could still nip and tickle. She hooted as I squealed, but then, in pure self-defense, I released my grip on Conor, who like the boss-ass girl dad he was becoming, immediately retreated.

Switching that same clasp, I tugged her close to me then used my grip on the backs of her thighs to roll us onto the sofa in a backward tuck.

In the glow from the Christmas tree lights, her delight glittered in front of me. And even on the days like today, where I felt as if I'd failed her because school bored the fuck out of her, I bathed in her happiness. In the love I'd never expected to feel for a not-so-small-anymore human. A love that let me realize I had so much more to give—in her own way, she'd gifted me Niall and Benji.

Amused by her squeals, I twisted her around and tickled her until she howled, "UNCLE! UNCLE! UNCLE!"

Only then did I stop. "No more talk of 'no kiss' jars? It'd be a crime to stop kissing that face, Kat."

Cheeks hot pink and eyes bright with her laughter, she chortled. "No more kissing—"

Another howl escaped her as I started back up again.

"FINE! No more jars. UNCLE! No more jars!"

"Oh, good!" I paused. "No more jars. Period?"

She squirmed underneath me. "I hit my target."

"You did?" I arched a brow because something wasn't adding up. "No way you have enough funds for a trip to Lapland for two adults and three kids."

"Feel free to keep swearing, Star. I'll gladly take the donations."

"Nice try. Where's the money going, kiddo?"

Her eyes dropped from mine. "I saw an ad on TV."

"You did?" I flopped beside her and snuggled her as I asked, "What kind of ad?"

"One about donkeys. Did you know their hooves grow really big and they can't walk and if they walk anyway, it leads to malformations in their legs?!"

"I did know that, baby," I admitted on a sigh.

When Conor plunked his butt on the coffee table, we shared a look. "You gave all your fund to the donkeys?"

"Well, they wouldn't take cash, but I didn't think you'd mind if I took one of your credit cards—"

"How the heck did you get that?" I demanded.

"Oh, well, Dad left his wallet on that tray in your bedroom. I put the money I earned in his wallet. I promise!"

"You're not supposed to touch our credit cards." Not after the *last* time—I'd been stepping on Legos for months because, and I quote, "Benji needed them." "Why didn't you come and talk to me first?"

"Because you were muttering about making the best cracker in the universe and the tool in your hand was smoking. I didn't want to distract you."

"Dad was in the gym."

"I yelled his name but he didn't answer."

"How loud did you yell?"

"Plenty loud enough," was her quick retort.

A smirk creased Conor's lips. "Do we agree that you don't use our cards again, Kat?"

"Of course." Her gaze cut to me. "But what if the donkeys need more cash? It's Christmas, Mom. Mary used a donkey. Everyone knows that. People should be nice to them."

"People should be nice to *all* animals, Kat."

"I only had so much money." Her lips pursed. "You're rich, Daddy. You already said so."

A soft sigh escaped me. "Is that why you wanted to start a 'no kiss' jar?"

"You two are always kissing. I'd be rich really fast. Then all the animals could be safe and have pedicures and stuff."

"Not sure that's what they— Never mind." Conor ran a hand through his hair. Honestly, he never looked sexier to me than when he was troubleshooting our kids' problems. "But we can figure something out, Kat. They do those programs where you can adopt animals."

"Oh, neat! How many can I adopt?!"

I'd have laughed if he hadn't walked straight into that one.

"Yeah, Conor, how many can we adopt?"

His eyes widened to borderline comical levels. "Ummmm..."

It's not like I could be mad at this. My kid, the cheeky monster, had given all her money away to some donkeys. Her heart was so fucking big that the idea of her growing up and someone hurting her messed with my head.

I tugged her into a tighter hug, just because I could and just because hugs with Mom would eventually stop being *cool*, and I mumbled, "We're open to negotiations."

"You are?" Kat squeezed me back. "Yaay!"

The rest of the evening involved us looking into which animals Kat could adopt, all while we huddled into first Benji's room and then Kat's to decorate their personal Christmas trees.

By bedtime, their trees were up, we'd played in the pool for a half-hour, Kat's voice was hoarse from talking, Benji had exhausted his encyclopedic knowledge on all things donkeys—why the kid knew so much about donkeys, I had no clue—and I could tell from Conor's expression that in our near future, the O'Donnellys would be opening an animal sanctuary in some shape or form.

Undoubtedly, it'd be dismissed as a tax write-off that had great optics, but there was no way the heartbreak in my man's eyes as we explored animal charities had anything to do with good PR and tax management.

The apartment was always quiet when Katina and Niall fell asleep. Benji had a quieter disposition, so the volume didn't shift that much around him and, ironically, he usually contained Kat's chaos. Just like tonight. Instead of her talking *our* ears off, she'd talked *his* off, and he'd come up with a barrage of info that had fed her ideas.

But with them all in bed, and the silence of the apartment encroaching, it never failed to put me on edge.

That was the double-edged sword of motherhood, I'd found. You fucking craved silence but never truly trusted it. And the more kids I had, the deeper my anxiety grew.

Not just because I was terrified I was fucking up, but because I wanted to make sure they had the best childhoods I could give them.

It was enough to trigger an anxiety attack, so like the smart woman I could sometimes be, I took the break as it came and went looking for my personal Valium once I'd finished bedtime with Benji.

Having figured he'd be working, I'd scoped out our office first, but he was standing against the wall of windows in our bedroom, a tumbler of whiskey in his hand as he stared at the skyline ahead.

Winter had come to NYC in all its glory. Snow tumbled in soft eddies at the moment, but earlier, visibility had been a nightmare. From this height, I could see white stuff doused Central Park, and I didn't even want to think about how cold it was.

A whole-body shiver rattled loose of its own volition as I stepped beside him. My lips curved when his free arm lifted and he automatically looped it around my shoulders.

It was easier to read his expression in our reflection, so I just rested my head against his side and stood there, enjoying the harsh contrast of the miserable night beyond with a warm and cozy one in here.

Still, my mind raced.

I knew Aurora De Laurentiis ran some kind of shelter, and I made a mental note to donate because nobody should be outside in *this*.

"You did a great job with her."

I glanced at him. "She did it herself."

"Nah."

"Yes."

"Naaaah."

I grinned but found myself quietly proud of his compliment. "Your ma thinks she's a nightmare."

"That's because she's a round peg and Ma's all square holes."

"Your poor father."

"Don't even go there!"

"You laughed first!"

"It was instinctual!"

"Well, don't blame me."

His snicker warmed my heart, especially because I felt the release of tension in him. My teasing had loosened him up. Something a kiss to the crown of my head only confirmed.

"I can see the cogs working from here."

"Huh?" He peered down at me. "Oh, nothing."

Hmmm.

"It'd be great optics." I helped him along.

"What would?"

I quirked a knowing brow.

His smile was sheepish. "I thought about couching it as a tax break."

"Of course you did."

"We could have parties. Rachel Laker does. You know. Those big galas."

"We could." I deserved a prize for not snorting like a loon.

"The O'Donnelly Petting Zoo." He chortled. "Nobody would ever think that someone who owned a petting zoo would have mob links."

"Wait until Shay's twenty-one next year and then have him establish it on his birthday or something. Frame it as him giving back to the community. It'll fuck up the SEO on his name. We can build toward that. Make sure we have pigs there too."

His lips pursed. "Just in case there are any references to our pig farms? Good thinking."

"Not just a pretty face over here."

"Gorgeous face," he corrected.

"So long as you think so."

"No." His tone shifted, turning oddly serious. "You need to think it because it's the truth. You're fucking beautiful, Star. Say it."

Because he rarely used that voice on me, my brows lifted. "I'm fucking beautiful."

He dipped his chin. "Now, say it like you mean it."

I hated how predictable my body could be around him. That voice, his urgency, the demand, the meaning—they combined and triggered the faintest stirrings of a blush.

That fecker.

I released a huff. "I'm—" I paused. Knew sarcasm or snark would get me nowhere with him. "I'm beautiful."

He twisted and cupped my chin, using his thumb to direct the soft pad as he gently tilted my head back. "Not just beautiful. Immaculate."

"Hardly."

"I see what no one else does. I see the real Star. And you are. A fucking gorgeous woman. And a wonderful mother—"

"Hardly," I croaked out, wondering how he always knew where the dark shadows of anxiety trespassed in my soul.

"A fantastic mother. The mother our children deserve."

With me melting, the height difference between us went to war with my synapses. I could feel my breathing quicken and my heart race. Softness curled inside my being, overtaking the hard shell that I used to get by.

Only he brought this out in me.

Only he made me crave *this*, him, instead of wanting to run for the hills.

I sucked in a breath that smelled of his new aftershave—a faintly incense-like aroma the kids had bought him because Katina had said his other one was for old men. This scented heady and warm and spicy. It slithered through my olfactory system, laying claim to that sense too.

Gently, he shuffled me forward until my back pressed into the window. The cool glass contrasted greatly with the wall of heat in front of me.

His eyes, so sharp usually, wicked humor and intelligence evident for all to behold, were soft with love.

For me.

It still boggled my mind that Conor O'Donnelly loved me.

All my battered and abused and broken and volatile edges didn't matter to him. He loved them because he loved me.

When I swallowed, a hungry cast seemed to mask his features. I wasn't surprised when his lips caressed mine or that he kept it gentle at first.

Soft brushes here and there. Mostly pecks. Innocent but filled with promise. Tenderly, he nipped on my bottom lip before laving it with his tongue. Instinct had me parting them, and he swept right in.

I shuddered as he breached every defense I had—emotional and physical—but I opened up to him.

Willingly.

When his tongue traced mine, toying and teasing, I followed. I *played*. I let him steal my breath, but only so that I could surprise him by twining them together and encouraging the battleground to shift to his mouth.

He groaned the second I did, and his erection branded my stomach because he'd switched into sweatpants post-swim and that meant I felt *everything*.

I delved between us and ran my fingers over his tip, concentrating there to drive him wild. His breath stuttered and his kiss faltered, but that was more than fine.

Just experiencing him react to me, his response, lit me up like a firework display. Nothing empowered me more than this gorgeous genius shuddering at my touch.

The jersey fabric grew damp from pre-cum, which told me he wasn't wearing underpants, and fuck if that didn't get *me* wet too.

I kept my touch light. His response was anything but.

Pushing our foreheads together, I bit his bottom lip as I tugged the waistband of his pants down and dragged his cock free.

One stroke of my palm over his length and he released a guttural groan that had my core pulsing in response.

When I sank to my knees, he grabbed me by the elbows. "Where are you going?"

"Where do you think?"

He huffed, but then with that wiry strength that often fooled me, he lifted me by the damn elbows and carried me to the trunk at the foot of our bed.

"Stay there," he ordered.

Though I blinked, he nodded and traipsed over to the closet after tucking his cock away.

When he returned with a vibrator, I laughed. "Is this one of yours?"

He scoffed. "Of course it is. I'm not letting you have anything but the best."

"I wondered where Lorelei's gifts went."

"Savannah's Mom can go to hell. *My* woman uses *my* toys."

His woman shuddered. "Is that my Christmas gift?"

"One of them."

I could feel the low-level burn begin. Just thinking about what this toy would do had warmth arcing through my body.

And he saw it too.

A cocky smirk creased his jaw, but he didn't say anything. To distract *from* that smirk, the wise man threw his hoodie off and then tugged down his sweats.

While I enjoyed the show, he dropped to his knees in front of me and carefully unfastened my jeans.

I wiggled to help him remove them as well as my panties and then tossed off my thin sweater before unhooking my bra.

Biting my lip, I watched as his gaze tripped all over me. Every inch received an appreciative glance. It was insane to be this wanted. This desired. I'd never known anything like it in my life, and it always made this so easy.

I rarely worried about the shadows of the past with Conor because he made everything brand new, and it was always enhanced by the knowledge that he'd put me on a very high, very stable pedestal.

I'd never be knocked off it. That level of certainty was a faith I had in only one person—him.

"You are so fucking perfect," he rasped, merely confirming where my racing thoughts had taken me.

I watched him study my cunt and knew that he could see the beginnings of arousal. His knuckles ran over my folds, one gently circling my slit before he tilted his hand and rubbed my clit.

"What does the next miracle toy do?" I released on a sigh as my back arched.

"It has a sucking motion—"

"Oh, I've seen those."

He sniffed. "You haven't seen one like this. It flutters back and forth too—"

"Like a lick?"

"Yes."

"And what do you intend on doing while that toy does all the work for you?" He eyed my tits, and I ahhhed. "Now I understand."

"Chef's perks?"

"You're not cooking anything."

"No, but I made you something infinitely unique," he demurred before fluttering his tongue over my clit.

The stirrings of pleasure began to awaken inside me. "So, you made a toy *just* for this?"

"I'm selfless."

"Oh, yeah."

"If you knew how many prototypes I burned through, you'd realize how selfless I am."

It was my turn to smirk. "Okay, I'm convinced. Who gets to come first?"

"If you don't, then I'll throw it out."

My eyes bugged. "You're such a perfectionist."

"If it doesn't blow your fucking mind, what's the actual point?"

"I can't decide if you're upselling or downselling this."

At my wry tone, he beamed. "Only one way to find out."

I studied the contraption, unsurprised that it didn't conform to any of the typical sex toys I'd seen on the market. The little sucker thing was different, and I could tell he'd taken my request for a harder edge on one side because I liked to feel the vibrations intensely on my clit. He'd also moved the power button from where it had been on the last few he'd created, and it weighed barely anything once he placed it in my palm.

Seeing his excitement and getting the idea that what I was about to experience would be life-changing... I hit the power button.

Immediately, my eyes widened—and that was just in the palm of my hand.

"Holy fuck!"

"Yeah. I had to be careful. I don't want to cause nerve damage from the vibrations, so make sure you hold it here."

I followed his instructions with a shake of my head.

"Now, press on it until it's the lowest vibe so you can build up to that level."

I blinked. Again. But did as he said. The softer level packed more of a punch than any toys Lorelei had ever gifted me.

He stared at me with an expectant air, and releasing a heavy exhalation, I rubbed the tip of the device over my clit.

My eyes widened before immediately shuttering. My brows furrowed and I uttered a deep, deep moan that bordered on *cleansing*.

A guttural sigh escaped me next as my hips jolted back, then forward as I rode the device.

Only when the early flutterings of release hit me did he murmur, "That's it, baby. Take your pleasure. Go on. Fuck me, you're so hot like this."

My throat bobbed as I keened, "Conor."

He grabbed my free hand and entwined our fingers. "Get it, Star. I want to see you come. I want to see that relief in your expression as you shoot off into another stratosphere. Keep your eyes on me, baby? Please."

A click sounded in the back of my throat as I did what he asked. And those chestnut eyes, bright with excitement and need and arousal, took me over the edge.

The vibrator was everything he'd promised and more.

But it was that *look*.

Fuck.

I sobbed through the orgasm. It was that fast, that intense, that powerful. It made my whole fucking being shudder in response to it.

"Conor," I moaned as my whole sex contracted.

The flicking and the sucking thing didn't just take my clit into consideration, but around it too. It was all-encompassing. Like pleasure was inescapable. Inevitable.

As I soared and flew free as per his damn request, the only complaint I had was it couldn't beat his cock inside me.

When my hips bucked upward and I jerked my hand to the side, giving me a break, he took the toy from me and switched it off. The sound of my panting breaths was overly loud in the bedroom now that the soft hum from the toy was no more.

"What the hell, Conor?" I whined. "Holy fuck. My whole body's tingling."

Excitement stared back at me. Seriously, his whole face glowed like the Christmas trees in the TV room.

"You need to sell that. Now. For women's sakes the world around. If I didn't have you, I'd never need a man with that freakin' thing."

His grin was wider than the Cheshire cat's. I traced it with my fingers, shaping his lips in appreciation. "Can't beat you. Never you."

He kissed my fingertips. "Want to see the attachment?"

I knew my eyes were back to bugging—extra wide this time. "Do I?"

"Oh, yeah. You do."

"Fine," I rasped, a touch hoarsely.

That orgasm... Wow.

When he disappeared then reappeared, I finally realized how hot he'd found that whole thing. Conor wasn't really a watcher, but I knew he dug seeing me use his toys.

His cock liberally leaked pre-cum.

Bright red and flushed like he was close to orgasming without me even goddamn touching him.

This man.

My mouth watered with the desire to taste him, but that wasn't what he wanted. Nah, he craved something else.

I glanced over the attachment and snorted when I realized what it was. "Hands-free device?"

"Hell, yeah. It should change the sensations."

I whistled. "Well, I can't imagine."

"Me either. I don't have a G-spot in the same place as yours."

That had my mouth dropping open. "Conor?"

"Yes," he muttered as he fiddled with the doohickey and screwed in the attachment.

"Did you use this toy on yourself?"

"An early prototype," he dismissed.

"And you didn't let me watch?!" I shrieked.

He paused in his actions. "I was experimenting—"

"Yes. And that's the kind of thing I'd like to see!"

"But it wouldn't have been a surprise—"

"Fuck surprises." I folded my arms under my tits. "Next time, you'll damn well invite me to the party."

His lips twitched. "Okay, boss."

"Like this is news to you," I derided before biting the inside of my cheek. "Wow, that must have been hot."

"Blew up like a geyser," he agreed with a snort.

"Ugh," I whimpered, reaching down and rubbing my sensitive clit. "Can't you use it now?!"

"Not really. I changed it too much." He pointed to some of the toy's features before rolling it around between his hands. "These weren't here before. It was a more unisex device."

"Then, for Christmas, you make that and we can each use one together."

His nostrils flared. "I can do that."

"Good. And don't forget that any experimenting, I want to see. You don't get to be all Mr. Inventor without showing me the perks too!"

"Noted." His voice lowered. "Ready?"

"Fuck. No. But also, yes. So, this is better?"

"Not better. Different."

I quivered. Literally. "Okay."

My whole body prickled with expectation as he smoothed his fingers over my slick folds. "You fine with me playing?"

"You know it," I said, almost embarrassed when the words hitched in the middle.

Another shudder wracked me at his careful touch, as if he knew it wouldn't be hard to take me over the edge again.

I sucked in a breath when the mindblower breached my entrance. It wasn't like one of those rabbits or a dildo. It had a funny shape that I couldn't begin to comprehend what had made him develop it, but it sank into me with pleasing fullness.

"Ohh, it's warm," I mewled.

"The material warms up with friction."

"That's why you were rubbing it between your hands?"

He hummed. "You told me once toys were cold."

"Oh, fuck. Conor. You're perfect," I warbled as he flicked on the power. I couldn't even be mad about his chuckle, not when he deserved it.

If the device had blown my mind before, this was going to wreck my body.

The sensations shuttled along my nerve endings until I was panting within seconds of him hitting the button.

It was warm. So warm. Tingling but with a solid buzz that murmured through to my soul. That murmur built. Slowly but surely until every inch of my channel felt it. The little bumps he'd shown me earlier settled into place, and so did the notches on his doohickey par excellence until I could feel my eyes rolling back in my head as the welter of sensation overtook me.

That low-level, incessant buzz rumbled into being until my whole lower body was in on the action.

He pressed something that turned it down and I blinked at him. His knuckles ran along my bottom lip before he sucked them into his mouth.

When he stood, I grabbed his hips for support because even at a lower setting, it was somehow all the more insidious.

A different kind of intensity.

Seeing as I'd rocked forward, the whole thing shifted inside me, directly impacting my clit.

My muscles contracted and I came.

Just like that.

So simple. So complex.

No short, sharp release.

But slow and delicious and all-encompassing. Sweet. Like an orgasm with *him*. My toes curled and my fingers dug into his hips as I drew him closer to me because holy fuck, my man deserved a reward.

Overwhelmed and overwrought and over-everything, I whimpered. "Conor."

His name was all I could say. Again.

Because he blew my heart wide open.

His smile wasn't smug, just happy. He didn't ask me if it was good. He didn't need to.

His hand stroked through my hair as he let me come down. Now that I'd had two orgasms, I was slaloming into recharge mode. I had no idea how he'd hard-wired my body, but thank fuck he had.

With the toy humming away, I released my hold on his hips and cupped my tits together. When he eagerly shuffled nearer, I pressed him between their pillowy softness.

His raw groan matched my earlier one, but it hit deeper because I knew he was ready from watching *me* get off.

And it was insane and delicious and made me shiver in a way that had nothing to do with a sex toy that his genius had literally created.

All that pre-cum lubed up my tits as he fucked them, hips pumping as I lowered my head and made sure to suck on his tip with every thrust.

He kept it slow and low-pressure and all the while, he growled shit like, "You are so fucking perfect, Star."

"God, your mouth. Your fucking mouth."

"You are so hot. God, you're my fucking everything."

"How are your tits so perfect? I fit between them like they were made for me. You are so gorgeous. Look at you. Jesus. Just fucking look at you—"

Then, my wily man pulled another ace from the deck...

I heard the click before I registered what it was.

And the vibrator's intensity shot up in response.

He had a remote!

I sucked harder on his cockhead as a result, and within seconds, he was pumping through the tight purse of my lips as he exploded inside me while my entire being went haywire.

My G-Spot wasn't just activated. It flew into hyperspace!

As he roared my name, I sobbed around his cock as the most wicked and wildest of climaxes hit me.

I wasn't surprised when my pussy muscles contracted so hard

that I pushed the vibe free. Nor was I surprised when I felt the soft spurt of my release either.

I let go of my tits to blindly reach for the toy, and after flicking the button, there was blessed silence.

Holding his cock in my mouth, I heard his heavy breathing, but mostly I was focused on not passing out.

It was there—right at the edge of my consciousness.

I dug my hands into his hips again, nails biting into him as I struggled to stay awake while my brain urged me to soar free.

A lifetime later, hours or minutes might have passed, I realized I was in bed. Conor tucked around me. Swaddled in blankets.

And, fuck, I was crying.

He stroked my hair and held me so close that I felt him in my soul. Soft hums and gentle kisses pressed wherever he could touch.

When I released a sigh, he murmured lightly, "Thank fuck. You scared me."

My mouth worked but I only managed to whisper, "I think I met Jesus."

A soft chuckle twirled and swirled into the atmosphere around us, further couching this whole thing with an intimacy that I'd never expected.

"You like it?"

"You get that on the market, stat," I rasped. "Women deserve to feel that. They can't have you, but they can have your mind. I'll let them."

More soft laughter.

"Call it the Fecker. They won't believe it." I shivered. "Until they experience it."

Feeling wrecked and reborn, I twisted in his arms so that I faced him.

Cupping his cheek, I whispered, "You're the perfect one, Conor. I don't know what I did to deserve you, but... you know I love you, don't you?"

Happiness beamed from him. "I love you too."

"And thank you."

"For the toy? You're welcome."

I kissed his chin. "Nah. For the extra soundproofing on this bedroom last year."

Closing my eyes, reveling in the sounds of his laughter, I pressed my forehead against his pec and felt him shift. Immediately, I glanced up and saw him drag his phone over to his side.

We never slept at the same time. Ever. One of us remained awake at all times to keep the spinning plates we managed on the daily in orbit. So I mostly felt relief when I saw him checking his programs on his cell.

It allowed me to close my eyes again.

It let me rest.

Because knowing he watched over the world while I slept in his arms?

That meant I was safe.

Our kids were safe.

And that the world was too.

So I allowed myself to succumb.

With him, sleep was possible.

With him, I'd slowly begun to accept, *anything* was possible.

SEVEN

WHEN THE ELEVATOR door opened on the first floor and I saw Savannah standing there, the burden of being an O'Donnelly shifted off my shoulders.

She did that to me—every time. It was why I fucking loved her so much. She brought so much goddamn happiness to my life that I knew, no matter who was right or wrong, I was always the asshole for creating that air of misery around her.

Her eyes warmed when she realized I'd been coming up from the parking garage, but she stepped into the elevator with a hesitation that crushed my heart.

That hesitance said, 'Does he want me in here with him? Should I wait for the next?'

Like she wasn't the most important person in my life.

Fuck.

"I was wrong."

She shuddered.

"Little one?"

Was that my voice?

That raspy, husky plea?

"I'll do better."

She peeped up at me, but whatever she saw, maybe my goddamn devastation, had her rushing toward me. I immediately opened my arms, and she hurled herself into them.

As the doors closed behind her, I tightened them around her upper back and pressed my lips to the crown of her head, closing my eyes in relief at her proximity.

It never sat right with me if we were at odds. Not just because I wanted peace in my home after dealing with the bullshit outside of it, but because Savannah was relatively easy-going.

"I hate it when we fight," I admitted gruffly, then I smiled when she tunneled between the flaps of my peacoat, getting as close to me as she could.

"I don't like it either, but I especially don't like it when I don't understand *why*."

My gaze caught our reflection.

I saw the strain in my expression, the fatigue from all the hours we'd been putting in recently, the bruises from the punches Brennan had managed to land, but mostly the exhaustion from a night spent without her in bed beside me. And I saw that same fatigue etched into her beautiful features.

Our codependency came as a shock.

I never imagined I'd become the type of guy who struggled to fall asleep without the warm weight of my wife at my side.

But I was.

Appreciating her affection, I stroked my hand over her back to instill patience because I struggled to find an answer. Even with Camille's advice, I found a response difficult to formulate.

"I have a gift for you," I ended up saying.

"You didn't need to buy me anything."

"I know you can buy whatever you want, but you'll appreciate this."

As much as she enjoyed presents, Savannah wasn't afraid to buy them for herself. Flowers included. It wasn't even a prompt. If she wanted something, she didn't mess around.

Self-denial wasn't a trait my wife suffered with.

"I don't want it if it means you won't explain what happened." Frowning, her fingers traced a cut on my cheek. "I don't want to fight with you, Aidan. There's bickering and sniping and we're good at that. But fighting? You froze me out."

"I overreacted."

"You don't say."

"Information is my currency, Savannah. It's how I keep *you* safe. My family safe. My people safe. But I hadn't heard anything about an animal-fighting ring. Not a fucking thing." I gritted my teeth. "Maybe it was ego, maybe it was just fear. I'm not sure which. But your question hit me on the raw.

"That's not on you. That's on me. And I'm sorry. You've always been able to come to me with questions and that'll never change. I didn't mean to freeze you out. That was a negative reaction to me not knowing about something that could impact our family's security. One small hole in the information I collate means a chasm might be waiting for me and I freaked out."

She blinked. "And if it happens again?"

"I'll tell you I can't answer right now but that I'll look into it and get back to you, so come and sit on my dick until I can give you the info you need."

"That sounds like a very good response," she mused, a smile dancing on her lips. "Especially the last part."

"I'm trying, little one. You might not have noticed, but I've been shutting out work once we're home—"

"I noticed. I didn't question it. Just enjoyed the change." She pulled a face. "Honestly, I feel bad because I'm not sure when the change happened or what triggered it." She linked her hands around my waist. "Why *did* you?"

"I missed you and Third." At her surprised gasp, I shrugged. "It happened at Halloween. I got home one night and you'd decorated the place with all those godawful pumpkins—"

"Hey! I hand carved each of them—"

"I know, darling," I said wryly, dotting a kiss to her temple. "I'm not sure it's your forte."

"Charming!"

"I came home and they were up, and then I came back and they were down. Each time, I found you in bed, curled up asleep, Third cuddled into you. I didn't see you make them, put them up, or take them down. Didn't see you or Third enjoy them. And what I did see was you asleep. I missed it all. Breakfast and dinner and everything else in between.

"So, I set myself limitations. I can't always make it back. There are fires that need extinguishing that I'm integral to, but I won't ever let it go so long again. And when I *am* home, my brothers and crew know to fuck off." Wryly, I tacked on, "That's why there'll be time for you to sit on my dick before I get you the info you requested."

"You did that because you missed us?" she whispered.

"Baby, I wouldn't have married you if I didn't want to be with you. I would have carried on fucking half the city's socialites if that's what I wanted. But I didn't. I wanted to come home to you. I wanted to sleep with you. I wanted to see you in the morning and late at night. It wasn't enough to just fuck *anyone* when you're all I want.

"I didn't tell you I love you because that's what you do when you get together. I mean it. Every word, every time."

Her bottom lip trembled. "I love you too. So much." Her hands gripped my turtleneck sweater at the back. I'd say she wanted to strangle me if love wasn't shining out of her eyes. "I love being with you too, and I love seeing you last thing at night and first thing in the morning."

A smile kicked up the corner of my mouth. "You just saying that?"

"No. I wouldn't have married you either, Aidan, if I didn't want to be with you. I was fine on my own. You know I'm independent. I don't need you to be with me 24/7. I've never needed that. And not just because of my work, but because I enjoy my own company.

"But everything's better when I start and finish things with you, too, so I know what you mean. If I just wanted to get laid, I could." She smirked at my scowl, and I knew that was payback for my earlier comment. "You know what I mean. Why go out for a burger when I can have prime rib at home?"

"Isn't that my line?" I teased.

"No, it's Paul Newman's, but if the meat fits…" When I laughed, she shot me an impish grin. "And now, seeing you be a dad is just everything I dreamed of."

"Same with you, little one. You're such a great mom." I pushed my forehead onto hers. "Speaking of, where is Third? Ma's?"

"I dropped her off at Paris and Aspen's. They'll be going on tour with Mom and Dad and wanted to see her before Christmas."

My brows lifted.

We were alone.

I'd lie if my dick didn't twitch in hope.

She noticed too, but her smirk quickly morphed into a grimace as she cupped my cheek. "Do I want to know?"

"Fights are good for the soul sometimes. Brennan needed to get it out of his system."

"Oh, Brennan did, did he?" She snorted at my smirk. "Brennan's actually the most level-headed out of all of you. You should give him more credit."

"I do!"

"I said credit. Not workload." She rolled her eyes. "Is that how you're 'creating' more time for us? By dumping it on Brennan? Because that isn't fair to him, Camille, *or* Roman."

"No. I'm dumping it on my crew," I drawled, hooking my hands low on her hips. And it was a partial truth. Brennan had officially begun taking over my position as head of the Firm. "That's what I pay them for. I've expanded it too. Lucas is ready for more responsibility, and he can manage them and any excess workload.

"Brennan's a control freak. He'll find his own path." *He had to.* But he was so fucking stubborn, I knew that throwing him in at the deep end would be a surefire way to help him figure that out. Still, I needed to change the subject, so I cocked a brow at her. "Heard things got informative during afternoon tea."

She arched her brow straight back at me. "And?"

"And I was wondering if you'd like to go Christmas tree shopping."

Savannah stilled. "To an actual lot? Or to Nordstrom's?"

"The lot around the corner."

"Oh, wow. This is so Hallmark. Are you going to pin me to the truck bed and feast on gingerbread cookies with me?"

"If I'm feasting on anything, it's you. As for the Hallmark movie, I have no idea what that is, have no desire *to* know, and if you ever tell my brothers that we discussed them, I'll plead the Fifth."

She sniggered. "I thought you were allergic to Christmas trees and all things festive! Conor told me that you hardly ever put up a tree before we got married!"

"This is me." I grimaced. "Turning over a new leaf."

"Something funky's going on but—" From suspicious to beaming, she shot me a bright-eyed smile. "—I'll take it."

Savannah wiggled out of my grasp and looked at the elevator panel. "Oh, we haven't moved." At my chuckle, she grouched, "Can I help that you make me dumb sometimes? Looking all hot in that peacoat—"

I groaned.

"You know I love you in a peacoat. Don't tell me that wasn't intentional."

"If it was, it was wasted on you. You only just noticed!"

"Don't sulk." Her gaze scanned me up and down. "Have you already been to the lot?"

"What, no?"

"Why are you covered in dirt?" Her nostrils quivered as she

approached me and gingerly sniffed my coat. "You are! You're covered in dirt."

"Hardly covered," I protested, but I refused to admit to succumbing to a potato attack. I didn't doubt she'd find out eventually, but that was a conversation for another day. "Anyway, I'm going to look at trees. Does it matter?"

"I never saw you as a manual labor kind of guy, Aidan." She tapped a manicured fingernail against her bottom lip. "I like it."

A laugh escaped me as I hit the button for the parking garage. "Of course you do, little one."

"Hey! I mean it!"

"I bet." I snagged her hand and used it to drag her out of the elevator once the doors opened. "Come on. The lot agreed to stay open past five for us."

"What?! We're going now? Wait, is this my gift?"

"No. Later." I dipped my chin at Lucas and Cade when they approached me in the foyer. "All set?"

"Yes."

Savannah's eyes widened, but she greeted, "Hi, boys!"

Lucas smiled. "Hey, Savannah."

Cade waved.

Well aware the rest of my crew had spread out for this five-minute walk around the block, I took my wife to the lot and watched as she waded through the trees.

Because this was Savannah, of course she had opinions and a knowledge base to back it up.

After I endured a speech about why the Fraser was superior to the balsam, I pointed at the twelve-footer. "Which is this one?"

"Fraser."

"Fine, that one, then."

Savannah tutted. "We should inspect it first." She didn't wait for an answer, just bustled off, and I watched her fluff and prod and do only God knew what to the poor tree.

Twenty minutes later, we were back in our building and heading up to our apartment with a promise the tree would be with us later that evening.

"This is for you."

When I retrieved the leather-bound journal from my pocket, her eyes narrowed then practically zoomed in on the "1984" embossed in gold onto the front cover.

"Is that what I think it is?"

"Da apparently kept a journal. Most of them, he tossed out, but this one, he didn't. Ma found it when she was hunting for decorations in her storage container. She gave it to me and, well, I figured you'd like it."

I didn't mention that I'd dragged Ma to said storage container after my conversation with Brennan and Camille while my crew worked on encouraging the seasonal lot that sold Christmas trees to remain open for us alone.

She snatched the journal from me, gaped at it, at me, at it, at me, then she squealed. She squealed so fucking loud, I was pretty sure she hadn't *come* that loud. Ever. Then she was dotting kisses onto my face and she carried on squealing, "I have the best fucking husband in the world! Oh, my god, this is the best gift you've ever given me!"

What could I say?

My mob-obsessed wife was fucking weird.

Not long after that declaration, her mouth collided with mine.

As her tongue thrust between my lips, I wasn't altogether surprised that she moaned at my hiss. Brennan's ring had snagged my bottom lip when he'd jabbed me, but her tongue swathed over it, even prodded the tear because she was a kinky little shit.

Then, when I thrust my tongue back against hers, she yanked on my sweater, tugging on it and pulling at it as she struggled to drag it over my chest, ignoring the fact I still wore my coat. Her fingers finally found my abdomen and she groaned as she hit paydirt—my belt buckle.

Evading it, she dipped lower and unfastened my zipper. Before I knew it, she was sliding to her knees.

"Savannah," I rumbled.

She peered at me, pupils gluttonously wide, all the while shaping my cock, stroking it until I had to grit my teeth. "What?!"

"Never change."

Her lashes fluttered. "Don't worry, babe, I won't."

I hissed the second her tongue lashed the tip of my cock, tracing every part of it until I had to grab her hair, twine it around my wrist, and tug her head back. "Play. Nice."

She pouted, which was a fucking sight to behold because she did so around my dick, but then she sank farther down my length, sucking and laving the back of my shaft with little flickers that had the muscles in my thighs bunching as she tortured me.

So, this was how she'd get back at me.

I'd have closed my eyes if seeing her watching me didn't turn me the fuck on. She blew me like the pro she was—she'd learned every single thing that messed with my head and used it against me.

I could feel it. The torment growing, building, just waiting for me to explode.

For me to cave into what she wanted—for me to pin her down and fuck her.

My nostrils flared as she whispered her tongue tip over the base of my shaft now that she'd worked her way down. Then, she swallowed.

And that was it.

I couldn't fucking take another second more.

And there was no way I'd waste my seed on her mouth. Hell, no.

She groaned when I used my hold on her hair to pull her head back. Her lips, sore and red and wet, caught my eye as I loomed over her and pressed my mouth to hers. I captured her tongue and, unlike before, I took the lead.

I felt her submitting to me.

That such a woman, so fucking strong and powerful and independent, did that, always made me so incredibly grateful.

It bewildered me too.

That she hadn't thrown my ass to the curb already was a miracle in itself.

As I fucked her mouth, I dragged on the lapels of her coat and forced it down her shoulders. Once she was free, I grabbed a hold of her hands, pinned them behind her back, then pulled away.

She gasped. "Aidan!"

Still cuffing her wrists with one hand, I hit the elevator button to release us onto our floor. Snagging her coat with my foot, I kicked it into the hall as I ordered, "Walk forward, Savannah. Slowly."

Of course, she disobeyed.

She darted forward until she yelped as I dragged her back against me via her cuffed wrists. "Get on your knees, little one."

Her hands wriggled in my hold, but I didn't let up, just watched as she lowered herself, awkwardly, to her knees. Once there, I released them, then withdrew one of my knives.

From behind, I pulled on the collar of her sweater dress and nicked it with the blade before cutting it from her body. When it sagged around her arms in a limp puddle, I heard her panting breaths.

"Oh, my god." She whimpered as I sliced the sleeves off too, then cut her out of her bra and panties.

Now that she was naked in our front hall, I rasped, "Stay there," and stepped away from her.

"Aidan," she mewled, then her eyes widened when she saw where I was standing, dick in hand.

"Crawl to me, little one."

Her tits heaved at the command, but she obeyed. Of course she did. Savannah fucking loved it when I took charge of her chaos.

The writhing of her body drove me insane. Her curves arched and angled as she shuffled toward me. When I saw the glimpse of pain in her expression, I figured her knees hurt. But like she knew I was on the brink of ending this whole thing, she scurried faster toward me.

Lips pursed, I retreated another single step and opened the door.

She peeked through the doorway like she hadn't seen it in a lifetime—and not just this morning.

Her lashes fluttered. "Aidan?"

"We're going to break this bed so you can never sleep in it again, Savannah," I told her calmly.

Her eyes widened, then she screeched as I snagged her by the waist and hauled her bodily into my arms.

When I dropped her onto the bed, the mattress and unmade covers fluttered, but I ignored them as I finally got a hold on her tits. Squeezing them until she squealed, I growled, "Do you want to break this bed with me, little one?"

"*Please.*"

"Get on your knees again."

She swallowed. "Okay."

"Spread them wider," I ordered until I could watch her slit pulsing. "Look at that little cunt. So fucking hungry for my cock. For what only *I* can give you."

"Yes, Aidan. Only you," she sobbed.

"So fucking desperate for your husband's cock, aren't you?"

Her breathing hiccupped. "Yesss."

I dropped to my knees, grateful as always that my rehabilitated injury held up under the strain, and I leaned down and sucked a part of her ass cheek into my mouth. When I bit it, she squirmed, then hissed when I sucked it again. Another bite. Another suck. Another bite. Another suck. Then, I combined the moves until she bucked into me, moaning, "Aidan, please, please, please."

"I love those words coming out of your mouth," I rumbled, eying the hickey on her ass with satisfaction.

Spearing her with my thumbs, I watched her back arch as she shrieked in surprise. Then, of course, she rode them—my cheeky wife.

"You're used to bigger than that, little one."

"If you won't give me what I need, then I'll take it—"

I didn't let her finish that sentence.

I freed my thumbs, straightened up, snagged a hold of my cock, then stroked it over her slit.

Her keening moan imprinted itself on my senses as I thrust into her. Fast. Hard. I took a second to watch her cunt collapse around me, her pussy lips twitching and shimmying as she accepted my girth.

Then, I sucked my thumb into my mouth. It tasted of her and a sweetness that not even my favorite brownie could compete with. Cleaning it off wasn't my intention, just lubing it up.

I pressed it to the pucker of her ass and thrust that into her too, then pushed down so that every time I sank back into her, my cock and thumb met.

She twitched at the sensation and her arms collapsed from under her.

"Savvie?" I demanded in concern, pausing my actions to check in with her.

"Don't stop," she whined, fingers scrabbling from underneath as she rubbed her clit. "Please."

Shaking my head at her craziness, I took in the sight of her, that sinful curve to her back as I fucked her until she breathed my name, until her cunt trembled around me, until her muscles quaked with the intensity of what I alone could make her feel.

I persevered, fucking her harder to combat her orgasm, enjoying her keening wails of pleasure.

And then, I pulled out.

When she shrieked my name, I dragged the small bottle from my pocket, relieved by my own forethought even though this evening could have ended in disaster, and I poured it on her asshole, then thrust my cock into her ass.

A single pump later, I filled that tight channel overfull, and she screamed.

I closed my eyes and gritted my teeth, fighting the urge to come too, ignoring the need to explode so soon. But she surged into action, fucking herself on my cock, clenching down around me until I thought I'd go insane, and all the while, she pleaded:

"Oh, god, Aidan. Please. I need your cum. Fuck me. That's it. Fill my ass, please. God, I need you. Fuck me. Harder. Please. You're so big. Oh, fuck. Fuck!"

And because I'd made her a promise, I gave her what she asked for. Faster, faster. She tore at the sheets, ripping them from the corners, dragging at the comforter until I heard the renting of fabric.

With my feet firmly on the floor, fucking her into the mattress was easy until, *finally*, I pounded into her hard enough for the legs of the bed to creak and groan.

To that soundtrack, I exploded into her.

Grunting, I pumped until my balls were empty. Until she sucked me fucking dry. I carried on until my cum came back to meet me, until it bubbled up at our joining and she was a sniffling, whimpering mess that trembled around my cock.

Then I reached around to rub her clit until she soared again.

I groaned in agony at the exquisite tightness of her asshole but forced my eyes wide open so I could absorb the sight of my powerful wife on her knees for me, my seed spilling out of her, ruined and yet never more beautiful to me than at this moment...

My cock pulsed a final time as I retreated, but when I clambered onto the mattress, I heard a second ominous creak.

I ignored it.

"Just hold it there, baby," I urged before I sank back onto the mattress, encouraging her to find shelter in the nook of my throat as I let her come back to me, her small form flopping on top of me like her muscles no longer worked.

It was, however, much too much for the bed.

With a final creak and a yelp from her, we plummeted two feet to the floor.

When I felt her delighted giggle tickle the side of my throat, laughter burst from me too.

"You always keep your promises," she pealed off.

In comparison to the misery of this morning, the sudden relief of her being in my arms, in this fucking bed, and *laughing*—Jesus, I was so goddamn happy.

Still chuckling God only knew how long later, she wiggled then stretched, her legs shooting straight out as she pointed her toes. Then, she turned to me with gleaming eyes. "You've given me quite the task, you know?"

"What do you mean?"

"How is my Christmas gift supposed to compare to *this*?"

Further confirmation she was fucking crazy.

Still, I shook my head and smirked at her. "Baby, don't you know, you're all the gift I can handle?"

Her smile illuminated the guest bedroom that I'd decided I needed to erase from existence last night while I'd been alone in our super king, and, of course, like the wisest of men, I had to taste it...

EIGHT
TEXT CHAT

Aidan: I owe you, Camille. Thank you.

Camille: No need to thank me. Just don't be a shithead

Aidan: Working on it 💀

NINE

WITH MY APARTMENT ODDLY SILENT, I peered around for Gracie.

My wife.

I still got a kick out of saying that.

In French, English—anything in between.

"Gracie?"

"In here!"

"Narrow it down."

"It's an open-plan apartment, Liam," she sniped, as grouchy as ever. "Figure it out."

"It's December. You're supposed to be nice to me now."

"My contract as your wife never stipulated that. Not my fault you didn't read the fine print. Take it up with God." She looked up from the counter where she was—

"Holy shit. Are you making pierogis?"

"Like you said, it's Christmas."

As she tucked and plucked and stuffed the literal food from the gods, my mouth watered.

And not just over the dumplings.

She wore a pair of jeans that showcased her ass off to perfection and a small tank top that gaped at her breasts because she had tits made for motorboating. *I'd know*—I'd done it last night.

"I booked our flights home—"

"What?" I blinked at her.

"I don't just talk to waste air, Liam. Are you listening or what?"

If my dick got harder at her sniping, then that was between me and my underwear. "I'm listening. Flights. What flights?"

"Plane. Home. Unless you intend on driving to Winnipeg?"

"You're coming with me, right?" I asked warily because she was saying one thing, but her tone implied another.

"You mean after Kow just told me that he's going to convert my bedroom into a trophy room?" Her smile turned deadly. "Bet your ass we're going there. Squatters' rights, Liam. Squatters'. Rights. We're not leaving the bedroom at all!"

My lips parted. "We're not leaving your bedroom?"

"Nope. Fuck him!"

"And fuck you," I rumbled.

Her nose tipped up. "Yes. Extra loud."

I moaned. "Oh, *minou*. I know you're not trying to talk dirty to me, but fuck if it isn't working."

Her gaze caught mine and she huffed. "I'm mad, Liam. Too mad for an angry fuck."

"You're talking about all my teen fantasies coming true! Fucking you under your mom and dad's roof?! Holy shit. Christmas is coming earlier than *I* will."

She hooted. "Shut up."

"I mean it."

I'd billeted with the Bukowskis when I'd been a Montreal teen who'd signed in Winnipeg. For years, they'd become as close to me as blood... and Kow had evolved into my best friend.

The dipshit.

Considering Gracie's hate affair with her younger sibling, that made for awkward clashes, but fuck if I wasn't here for this one.

I sidled around the counter and looped my arms around her waist. She huffed when she felt my erection digging into her ass but kept quiet when I didn't actively make a nuisance out of myself.

"Why's he changing your bedroom anyway? I'd have thought Hanna would have something to say about that." The two got along better now, and Hanna rarely let her sons give Gracie shit.

"She did, but apparently it's Dad who agreed because it's the smallest bedroom. So I'm going to make sure that I hide all Mom's pierogis so he can't have any." She peered at me over her shoulder. "We're about to become Gremlins."

Snickering, I pressed a kiss to her cheek. "Gremlins who fuck?"

"Loudly, remember? Just to make *everyone* uncomfortable."

I whistled. *"Tabarnak, femme.* You're my hero."

TEN
TEXT CHAT

Star: I need your help

Aoife: Mine?

Star: We have to work on our mutual menfolk

Aoife: Gladly

Aoife: To what end?

Star: Destruction

Aoife: 😳

Aoife: What are we destroying?

Star: AI

Aoife: Huh?

Aoife: Think the horse's bolted, no?

Star: If Benjamim tells me one more time that a single prompt uses a bottle of drinking water in a world that only has water because comets landed on earth back in the day and that our source is finite, I'll scream

Star: So, we either destroy AI or I tell my kid I can't fix this

Aoife: Right, okay, what's the plan?

Star: You get onto Finn. Hell, I'll communicate with the others too. We all need to nag our respective men. If we do that, then they'll figure something out

Star: I'll come up with a way to make Shay look good. You know they're obsessed with the White House.

Aoife: True, if you make it look like eradicating AI will save human jobs then that's bound to work. Especially if Shay can spearhead a campaign or something

Aoife: Benji's upset, huh?

Star: His heart's too big.

Star: And I don't want to make it smaller by failing him

Aoife: We won't, honey. Maybe they can buy a data center or something?

Star: OMG! I know what to do! Conor was just complaining about how hard it is to buy Christmas gifts for Finn

Aoife: Hmm. It'd be better though if he didn't get it. Reverse psychology

Star: Holy shit. You're right! What does he need?

Aoife: His favorite tie pin lost a diamond

Star: Ordinarily, I'd feel it would be my duty to say 'First World Problems'

Star: But this works in our favor

Star: I'll tell Conor to get him that and then you work on making Finn hate AI

Aoife: You do know this isn't necessary, don't you?

Star: Huh?

Aoife: Well, they usually give us what we want

Aoife: Why don't we

Aoife: Ask

Star: Pfft. I knew I should have gone to Savannah. She's devious!

Aoife: Hey! That's not offensive. I'm pleased you don't think I am

Star: This is a multi-billion-dollar industry we're talking about dismantling, Aoife. WE NEED DEVIOUS

Aoife: 🙄

Aoife: Fine.

Aoife: But when they find out and give us puppy-dog eyes and tell us they'd have helped if we just asked…

Star: I'll let you say I told you so

Aoife: Precisely. 😌

ELEVEN

WHILE I PUSHED the cart down the produce aisle of our local grocery store and Jake pleaded, "Go faster, Daddy, please, please, please," from his seat within said cart, Aoife dumped an obscene number of carrots beside him.

They were the fancy organic kind, much like everything in this place. It was all wicker baskets and expensive cheese and deli meats. I couldn't complain—the darker environment, with its softer lighting, made Aoife's hair gleam and turned her into one of my walking fantasies. Watching her was always one of my favorite pastimes.

Until I saw what she had in her hand.

I froze in outright horror at the bag of loose greens she tossed on top of the organic, grown-in-special-shit carrots. "God, you're not making carrot and cilantro soup again, are you?"

"Because you asked extra nicely, I'll make sure there's enough for you."

"Cilantro is the devil's herb." I gagged.

"Says you. I love it. So do most of your family."

"It speaks of my love for you that I'm willing to kiss you *after* you consume it."

She snorted. "You're so melodramatic. We both know you'll do anything for a kiss."

"Do you hate it when I drink vodka?"

"Thank God the Irish in you won't let you drink it all that often." She bobbed her head double-time. "Vile stuff. And no, actually, soup hater—"

"Don't pout. I eat all the other soups you put in front of me."

"You're oddly critical about my soups." Her pout became more defined.

"Well, you know I can—"

"Yes, yes. Only eat it with my bread."

"What can I say? I have standards."

A smile danced over her mouth, making the corners of her eyes crinkle, and after checking that Jake was occupied with his cartoon and the toy dinosaurs he'd brought with us, seeing as I refused to treat the cart like a McLaren F1 car, I quickly leaned down and kissed her. Because her lips parted, I accepted the invitation and thrust my tongue against hers.

The soft moan she released had me stepping closer so I could slide my arms around her waist.

Her softness, as always, welcomed me home. I took a moment to indulge in her curves, then I teased her by nipping her bottom lip before laving it with my tongue.

When she hummed in delight, I tightened my hold around her as I—

"Excuse me! This is a grocery store. That *cannot* be sanitary."

Tension filled Aoife at the criticism, but I didn't let it bother me. I finished the kiss... slowly, softly. Just long enough to hear a disgusted huff.

Straightening and taking note of Aoife's bright red cheeks, I narrowed my eyes at the other woman who stood there, glued in place like she couldn't have easily walked past us, toe tapping against the floor.

Some people have to choose drama every time.

"If you haven't been kissed since the Reagan administration, just say so, ma'am."

"I beg your pardon!"

"No need to beg. I pardon you. Willingly. If you'll stop being the Grinch—that's the green, furry guy you see everywhere this time of the year—I can practice forgiveness."

"The nerve of—"

"I have plenty of nerve." I shot her my most charming smile. "But they're being worn thin by you. Now, you didn't have to interrupt an intimate moment between husband and wife. You didn't have to step outside today and *choose* to be a cunt, but here we are." She blanched. "So, you toddle off to whatever cave you came from, and I'll let you without bringing down the manager."

"I'm the one who'll visit the manager, young man!"

"Please do."

With a huff, the woman spun on her heel and stalked off. Her cane clacked with every step she took as she abandoned her cart in the center of the aisle.

Aoife burst out, "But—"

I lifted a hand. "No, Aoife."

Her lips pursed. "You do know she was wearing Chanel shoes?"

"Do I look like I give a damn?"

"She hardly came from a cave, Finn."

I shrugged. "Don't be classist, Aoife."

She stuck out her tongue. "You know she's old if she calls *you* 'young man.'"

"Well, that's nice!"

Her grin made an appearance. "I can't believe you called her a C-U-N-T!"

"Mommy, what's a See You En Tee?"

"That's what you pick up on?" Aoife cried, aghast.

I hooted. "Don't complain."

Her shoulders sagged. "Fair enough."

"It's just a joke, kiddo," I told him, just so he'd return to his cartoon.

Curving an arm around those slumped shoulders, I hauled her into me and pressed a kiss to her forehead. "This time of the year, love's what matters most, no?"

"True." She pulled a face. "We did kiss for quite a while, and I maybe, *probably* moaned louder than I thought—"

"Not long enough and not loud enough for me. This isn't 1843, baby. Jesus Christ. From her reaction, you'd think I shoved you onto the fridge and started eating you out!"

Her blush resurged. "Later?"

I snickered. "If my *wife* wishes."

She wafted a hand in front of her face, amusement and heat glinting in her eyes. "Right. Shopping. I still have loads to buy. Potatoes and broccoli and—"

"Why didn't we get this online again? I could kiss you in the kitchen without being accosted by octogenarians who need to get laid." I tapped my finger on the cart's handle. "I know a good gigolo service. Maybe that's what her poor family should buy her for Christmas? I'm sure they do gift cards."

Aoife, midway through sorting out herbs in a pile, turned to gawk at me. "Why do you know that?"

When she pointed to a bag in a bucket, I hefted the potatoes into the cart then nudged the Karen's aside when it got in our way. "Think about what my brothers do, Aoife." Her eyes flared. "Don't be sexist either."

"Finn!"

"What? Only women can do sex work and not men?"

Her mouth did a great impression of a puffer fish's.

"Remember that expression later," I teased. "Looks like a good time."

She whacked my Vicuña winter coat with a bunch of what smelled like parsley. "You did not say that!"

"I live to tease."

She squinted at me. "Why do you know these gigolos?"

"I don't. I know *of* them. That's not my bag. Why are you asking? Is my performance not up to snuff? Here was me thinking an orgasm a day kept the *gigolos* away—"

"This is what I mean! These two delinquents are disgraceful. Discussing such intimate, *private* topics in public. I demand you do something about it!"

The squawking drew my attention yet again, and when I glanced over my shoulder and found the old bitch and the discomfited manager, I merely raised a brow.

The man's eyes darted over to Aoife who, of course, blushed again—redhead's curse.

Garrett Lewis, the manager, immediately cleared his throat. "Apologies for disturbing—"

"Apologies! I ask you!"

He continued like the woman hadn't interrupted him. "I'll deal with this, Mr. O'Grady."

I slowly dipped my chin.

"Mrs. Vandersand, let me take you to our bistro and we can—"

"Your bistro? What are you talking about, young man?! I want to see these two hooligans thrown out!"

"Ma'am, Mrs. Vandersand, Mrs. O'Grady owns this store."

The Karen gaped at him. Then me. Then Aoife.

Because my wife was a saint, a literal saint, even if she had just made out that an orgasm a day wasn't enough, she peppered kindly, "Mrs. Vandersand, why don't you let Garrett take you to the bistro for a cup of tea to settle your nerves?"

Because the old bitch's face screwed up like she'd been sucking on lemons, I chose to disengage.

My wife didn't deserve to hear more of this outdated vitriol. I'd kissed her, not fucked her! I almost wished I *had* now.

Hell, if Jake weren't here...

As Mrs. Vandersand sputtered, at a complete loss for words, I pushed the cart away. "I'll be in to speak with you later, Garrett."

It took us reaching the second aisle in the store for Aoife to release a wheeze before she bent over and fell into a laugh/giggle combo that was beyond charming.

Because of its utter contagiousness, Jake ignored his dinosaurs and the show he'd been watching on Aoife's phone and started up too —his childish delight echoing around us.

"The nerve of some people!" Mrs. Vandersand declared, but I barely heard it over the laughter that bubbled around me.

With a wide grin, I half-leaned on the cart and watched my two favorite people laugh themselves silly.

When Aoife began rubbing her stomach, I knew the end of the fit of giggles neared.

"Something funny?"

She whooped. "Don't get me started again." Jake bounced in the cart, and she squeezed his cheeks and dotted kisses on them. "Daddy's hilarious, isn't he, little man?"

"I think I'm deadly serious," I countered, pleased by the megawattage of her resulting smile.

"Why don't I bring you grocery shopping with me usually?"

"Because I prefer to buy stores than produce?"

"That could have something to do with it." She reached behind me for a packet of stuffing—the kind her mom used and one she imported when I'd bought an upmarket grocery store under Aoife's umbrella corporation—the first of two in the city. "I can't believe I didn't put this on my list."

"I can't either. There'd have been a showdown over the table. That's the only brand Declan and Eoghan will eat since Star won the stuffing war of '23 using your recipe."

"I think I willingly forget," she mused. "Because you all drive me crazy with the reminders. If I have to hear about how Lena's makes Declan gag one more time, I'll lose my shi—sh for real."

"Nice save."

She eyed Jake, who hadn't picked up on the swear word and had returned to the annoying cartoon on her phone. "I thought so too."

"Eoghan will pack that away by himself." I studied the three packets in the cart dubiously. "You need more than that, babe."

"How many?"

"Two more. Minimum." Contemplating historic holiday dinners, I rubbed my chin. "You'll prepare the loaves the day before?"

"Don't I always?"

"Nothing beats your loaves, baby. Not even the stuff from the bakery."

"That's because I don't use your mom's recipe at the bakery."

My eyes widened. "You don't?"

Her smile turned sheepish. "That's your bread. Nobody else's. I use a tweaked variation for my customers."

I growled, "You're lucky we're in public or I'd *ruin* you right now."

"Already tried that once, mister." Her delighted laughter echoed down the aisle. "Look where that got us."

When I tumbled her into my arms, her laughter followed, so I vowed to show her later what her revelation did to me. "Is that a complaint, Mrs. O'Grady?"

"Not at all." She smirked. "That bread won you over—"

"Nah, baby, you did that by breathing."

Her amusement softened as she trailed the backs of her fingers over my jaw.

I tilted my head for better access and drawled, "Okay, I'll need one loaf to myself. Minimum. Only Jake can have my recipe. Not my brothers—"

"Finn," she chided around a giggle.

"—I don't know what you do to the turkey, but sweet fuck, that, the stuffing, your bread, and some mayo? Heaven. In fact, that'd be my death row meal."

"A turkey stuffing sandwich would be your death row meal?" she stated, tone dubious as she scanned the deli area for more items on her list and nipped my ass to get me moving.

"No. *Your* turkey stuffing sandwich on *my* bread." I patted my stomach when I saw her peering at the fresh turkeys. "I dedicate an extra hour in the gym in the run-up to the holidays for those alone."

"You'd think I didn't feed you on the regular!"

I curved an arm around her waist and hauled her into me again. "You feed me all kinds of sugar. No, I was wrong." I pressed a softer kiss to her lips. "*This'd* be my death row meal."

Her hands pressed against my pecs and she leaned into me. It came as a relief, actually. Aoife still got flustered by PDAs, and that Karen could have ruined it for her.

But, no.

She sighed into my mouth, head arching back as I deepened this kiss. When my tongue swept over hers, her fingers clutched at me and she broke away to breathe, "I just remembered why I can't take you grocery shopping."

"Why's that?" I pressed soft pecks to her cheeks and forehead and wherever else I could reach.

Aoife snuggled into me. "Because you're a menace."

"I live to menace."

"That isn't even a verb."

"You can check it out in the dictionary later." I nuzzled my nose into her temple, where the scent of her was sweet and clean and just *Aoife*.

Fuck, I loved her.

Some days, it felt like it exploded out of me.

I closed my eyes, just appreciating the moment, the intimacy in a fully public space. She relaxed into me, arms around my waist in a total hug that neither of us wanted to end.

Not even when Jake began shrieking.

Still, I tipped my head and saw why my kid was shouting—Garrett Lewis hovered at the end of the aisle beside a fancy basket of cookies.

A soft smile curved his lips, not in disapproval or embarrassment, more like understanding. When I'd looked into his background for the management role, I'd learned that not only was one of his kids a professional hockey player who played for our team, but he'd been married for thirty years.

With a soft squeeze, I released Aoife. "Everything okay, Garrett?"

He nodded but directed his answer at Aoife—smart man. She was his boss, after all. "Mrs. Vandersand might not be returning to the store, Mrs. O'Grady."

Aoife hitched a shoulder. "I doubt she'll be gone long. Did you see what was in her cart?"

"No, what?" I asked because Garrett looked as clueless as me.

She beamed at us. "Three of the extra-large packs of my brownies."

Slowly, I drawled, "And our nearest bakery is across the neighborhood." Proudly, I grabbed her hand and kissed her knuckles. "Creating addicts, one brownie at a time, darling."

"I know I'm one," Garrett admitted.

"Precisely." Her smile, as always, remained kind, but I saw the shark there. A shark that I'd help create—fuck, she was hot in business mode. "Now, I have shopping to do. I'll see you around, Garrett."

He said his farewells and drifted off as quietly as he'd shown up.

I turned to her with an arched brow. "Those brownies will win our family the White House."

She patted my shoulder and smiled.

But that smile?

Told me she agreed. She was just too modest to say so.

TWELVE

"SAVANNAH, is Camden in town and nobody told me?"

"Nah. He's in Japan, I think. Mom mentioned something about someplace. This fucking thing! Agh!"

"Informative as ever."

"It's the journalist in me."

"He's still on tour?"

"Yup. Why?"

"I dunno. I thought I saw him last week, that's all."

"How was Lapland?"

"Fucking cold."

It wasn't altogether odd for Star and Savannah to be up here, griping at one another, but I still glanced into the TV room anyway.

When I saw the knitting circle, I literally had to take a step back and then regretted it as I tripped over Beavis and Butthead.

What the fuck?

I retreated to the hallway.

The Twilight Zone?

Shook my head.

Psychedelic drugs?

Then I peered through the door again.

"Oh, stop fussing, Conor," Ma groused, proving where I'd gained my surveillance skills.

Totally inherited.

But, yeah. No tripping, no Rod Serling—just my woman, my mother, my sister-in-law, *and* my cousin.

<u>Fucking knitting.</u>

"I'm not fussing!" I shook my head again as I took in the scene. Somehow, the fact that Jennifer *didn't* have a pair of knitting needles made the most sense to me. "I've seen Star making—"

"Conor! Shut your trap! It's a secret," she yelled at me, her eyes promising a not-so-fun time as she shot me ocular daggers.

I held up my hands and quickly pivoted from "homemade explosives" to, "Making her Secret Santa gift and now you're all knitting?!"

"We're crocheting, actually," Savannah retorted, frowning at the very holey piece of fabric she discarded on her knee.

As for Star, the holes seemed uniform, but the way she held the hook in her hand reminded me of a goddamn weapon.

Jen leafed through one of Kat's *Teen Vogues* and shot me a desultory wave when she realized she'd caught my eye.

"What's happening here?" I asked her because she was the only one unarmed.

Star never willingly spent time with Ma, so this whole thing felt like I'd fallen down a black hole and had been spat out in Narnia after vacationing in Wonderland via a detour to Whoville.

"Lena is teaching them how to crochet, and I'm learning about the devolution of the Supreme Court."

"See, that's where my confusion stems from. You can already crochet, Star."

"I can, but Savannah can't, and I wasn't frickin' teaching her. She's a whiner."

"Hey!"

"Now, dear, it's fine," Ma chirped. "Everyone whines now and then. Aidan used to do it all the time when he and Brennan were small. My little whiner."

Savannah smirked at her fond tone. "I think I'll call him that later."

"Now, Brennan was my stoic one. Always scowling. Conor was a bit of a crybaby—"

"Ma!"

"What? It's true. He was on the breast for three years—"

"Ma, for fuck's sake!"

Star halted the craft of 'stabbing wool into knots.' "So, that's where the fascination started, huh?"

"Do not ruin breasts for me," I protested.

"That's where all men's fascination with tits starts," Jen derided, with a distinctive turn of the page in her magazine. "This isn't new information."

"It is for me!" Star jeered, but I saw the gleam in her eyes and knew I'd never hear the end of my ma's loose goddamn lips.

My ship would not be the one sinking!

So *what* I'd made her an orgasm machine for the express purpose of fucking her tits? She had banging tits! It was only sensible to worship at their altar.

"What about Eoghan?" Savannah huffed when she stabbed herself and not the wool or whatever disaster she attempted to make for one of my poor sisters-in-law. "And Dec?"

"Eoghan was very quiet. That was probably for the best. Things were hectic with five boys in the house at that point—"

"No shit, Ma."

"Aidan and Brennan helped a lot—"

"*Hit* a lot."

"They didn't!"

"They did. Knuckle sandwiches in exchange for peace and quiet."

Ma scowled over the shawl she crocheted. "You never said."

"I'm not a snitch! And when I cried—" My tone turned pointed. "—you called me a *crybaby*."

Though her cheeks pinkened at my wry tone, she harrumphed. "Declan was forever in the coloring books—"

"Until Da said they were for girls and threw them out—"

"Conor, you're aggravating me."

I rolled my eyes. "The truth stings."

"Conor!"

"Ma!"

It wasn't often that I raised my voice, but I wasn't about to let her paint a fairytale story about our upbringing in my own goddamn home. Some of it had been fun, some of it had fucking sucked, and some of it was downright brutal.

I wasn't complaining about this fact of life. But letting her spin her BS wouldn't serve anyone.

"It wasn't so bad, was it?" She sounded wistful and I knew she was thinking about the old days. The old *good* days. At least, in her mind.

"Not all the time."

She nibbled on her bottom lip and nodded, like she knew I conceded for her sake.

"Well, that conversation became gloomy hella fast," Jen mocked with a crisp turn of a page in her magazine.

Instead of answering, I stepped into the room and plunked myself beside Ma. I hadn't meant to give her a hard time, so the least I could do was sit next to her. Beavis did me a solid by snuggling up to her, and she cooed at him in delight.

Then, without looking at me, she passed me a skein of yarn, and my fingers did the talking as I began untangling it for her.

Man, it'd been years since I'd done this, but muscle memory pulled most of the slack.

"So, what are we making?"

"Can't tell," Savannah muttered, then stuck her tongue between her teeth as she concentrated.

"Something unrecognizable by the looks of it," Jen taunted.

"Fuck off and fuck you," Savannah countered, saccharin sweet.

"Crafting, ugh." Jen pulled a face. "That's for Easter—"

"How is Easter the time you give crafted gifts?"

Jen shrugged at Star's question. "Because you don't want to mess up the Christmas gifts. They're sacred."

"I wouldn't hate adding another gift tier to the holiday options," I agreed. "Birthday and Christmastime just aren't enough."

"Luciu tried to give out gifts at Thanksgiving. He doesn't get it."

"He's Sicilian, dear. Why would he? It's not a part of his culture. Do you know what?" Ma paused in her crocheting. "I hate corn."

My eyes bugged. "How do you hate corn? And what does corn have to do with crafting?"

"I do. I just decided. Your father loved it, of course. Always had me making corn casseroles, creamed corn, corn pudding, and corn-bread muffins—"

"No wonder you hate it." Jen turned green. "That's corn overkill."

"Exactly. No more corn for me," Ma declared. "There'll be none of it tomorrow, that's for certain."

I gaped at her. "No corn pudding?!"

"No. But I'll give Star the recipe."

"Gee, thanks, Lena."

"You're welcome, dear."

Either Ma didn't hear the sarcasm, or just ignored it...

"Heard about the vacation over the holidays, Lena." I could have kissed Jen in thanks for changing the subject. "Sounds neat. You're really going with Paddy?"

Jen had started calling Uncle Paddy *Dad*. Unless he pissed her off.

As I pondered what he'd done, Ma hummed. "I told him he could come if he packed a suit."

"Ah, so that's why Luc had to take him shopping last week?"

"Probably. I told him he was too damn old for a woman to hold his hand in a clothing store." Her scowl turned fierce. "And I won't be having him show me up. I also told him he'll have to shave everyday and none of that low fade nonsense Shay talks about. I asked Luciu to encourage Paddy into buying some hair gel. He'd better use it."

"What's the deal between you two anyway?" Savannah queried then, huffing, threw down her work. "I hate this so much. I'll never get it and I'm running out of time. Can you buy this shit online?"

"It's busy work, dear. Persevere. You'll come to enjoy it."

Savannah's expression said she doubted that very much.

"You can, but I'll tell the person you cheated," Star chirruped, forcing a grin out of me.

Savannah narrowed her eyes. "Payback's a bitch."

"*You'd* know."

"Girls!" Ma tutted. "No fighting. We talked about this earlier."

I'd have paid for ringside seats to watch *that*.

"As for Paddy and me, well, he's good for fixing things to walls—" Jen snickered at Ma's statement. "—and he eats what I put in front of him without much fuss, so I can cook for two instead of one. We have a lot in common—"

"Are you *together*?" Star asked.

All three women leaned in like they wanted to know.

I, on the other hand, *did not*.

"A woman has needs," Savannah concurred to my horror.

"She certainly does," Jen agreed.

Star hummed. "And Paddy takes direction well."

I stared at them, aghast, realizing they wanted my mother, my actual mother, to discuss her fucking sex life!

In front of me!

"He—"

When Kat yelled, "MOM! DAD!" relief hit me as Ma's head whipped over to the door, and I knew the distraction would sustain this conversation until I left the goddamn room.

"I'll deal with whatever's happening," I said quickly, jumping to my feet, dumping the ball of yarn on the floor in my haste to run into the hall as my dogs raced alongside me. "Where are you, Kat?"

"Kitchen!"

Of course, I soon found that was a lie.

"Kitchen? You meant war zone, right?" I gaped at the state of it. I didn't know what was more heinous—the conversation going down in my living room or FlourNam. "Is that flour on the ceiling? When did you even do that? I didn't know you were home!"

"We have to bring Christmas cookies into school tomorrow."

When Ren and Stimpy hissed at my dogs, I picked them both up and plunked them in their bed with the order, "Stay." Ignoring their whining, I wagged a finger and they settled down with a huff. The cats curled into balls on the table. With a battle momentarily appeased, I directed at Kat, "You do know we could have bought Christmas cookies from Aunt Aoife's bakery?"

"You're right." She whistled under her breath then flicked looks between the ceiling and the mess on the counter. "But that'd be lying, and Mrs. Bosko said we had to make them at home from scratch."

I never knew whether to be happy or not that Star, with all her espionage skills, had somehow passed on the need to always be honest to our daughter. Now, she could be sly. But invariably, a thread of truth could be found in whatever she said.

"Aunt Aoife could have prepared the dough on Sunday, and then we could have put them in the oven here at home. What have we told you about technicalities?"

She tapped a finger against her cheek. "That they equal victory?"

"Precisely." I added, "And that they're not a lie." Her biggest issue.

Her gaze dropped to the counter. "But what if I wanted to bake cookies with you?"

"Me or your mom?"

"Either." She hitched a shoulder. "Both. You."

I pointed to myself. "Me? You sure?"

Kat ducked her head. "It's fine if you don't want to."

"No, of course I do. I'm just not very good at from-scratch baking. Remember last year when Benji and I made brigadeiros?" I kept my tone light and teasing, sensing that there was something going on here. Her snicker-snort told me she remembered the chocolate sprinkle disaster. "Aoife's the go-to person for cookies."

She shrugged. "It's fine if they suck. I don't like Mrs. Bosko anyway."

I chuckled because that was such a "Star" thing to say.

Amused, I situated myself at the counter to wash my hands and grimaced when I saw how much flour dusted everything from this angle.

"Wow," I muttered, eyes on the hazy spotlights as I grabbed the kitchen towel and dried my hands off. "You made a real mess. I'm almost impressed."

"I didn't think it would be that hard."

"How were you carrying the bag from the pantry to the counter? Upside down? And why is none of it on you?!"

"Daddy!" she wheedled, but she made my heart soar regardless. I was mostly "Dad" now. Whenever "Daddy" came out, it always put a smile on my face. "Why do they make bags that big anyway?"

"I'm asking myself that question too." I nudged her with my elbow. "Okay, so what's on the docket?"

"Sugar cookies."

"Fine. You have a recipe?"

"I asked Aunt Aoife."

I grabbed the printout that she handed me and read the instructions. "We can do this."

"You sure?"

"Well, no. But you're in AP Physics and U.S. History and are designing a cantilever bridge for fun. As for me, I have the intelligence to keep up with your mother. We got this."

I glanced over the ingredients she'd set on the counter, took note of the offending bag of exploding flour, and set out bowls to weigh individual ingredients into. We began with sugar.

"Dad?"

I shot her a look as she grabbed a teaspoon and shoveled granules into the dish once we neared the right amount. "Yes?"

She kept her gaze angled away from me. "Shay and I aren't related, are we?"

Pondering the best way to answer that, I snagged the bag of sugar and fastened it with one of the clips Star insisted we use. The last time I hadn't, she'd left the clips all over my desk for a month. By the end, we'd had to dedicate a whole cupboard in the kitchen to bag clips.

"Well, you *are*. You're family. But genetically speaking—"

"Because cousins shouldn't intermarry," she prompted, and I thanked God she brought this to me and hadn't discussed this with her friends at school.

Again.

"—correct. You're not."

"So, it wouldn't be weird for me to have a crush on him?"

I blinked at her.

Why was she talking to *me* about this?!

I pondered calling in Star. Then, when she blinked back at me, I swallowed again.

Had the females in my family collectively decided to torture me today?

Hell, couldn't she have asked her sister about this? Alessa never even twitched at the random madness Kat spewed.

If my voice sounded strangled, so be it. "No, cupcake. It wouldn't be weird for you to have a crush on him. I think Freud said there was a phase in every child's development where they had a crush on their parents, so a non-blood-related cousin isn't strange at all within those parameters."

Her aghast expression had me sniggering. "You made that up!"

"Nope. Look online."

"This is why those shows exist. That Maury dude."

"I'm surprised you know about him."

"Mom made me watch a rerun."

"I didn't even know they had those," I said dryly as I grabbed the butter and sliced cubes of it into the bowl. Deciding I needed to change the subject, I mused, "I thought it was all cups."

"You mean weigh stuff out? Aunt Aoife says that baking by volume isn't easy when you're a noob."

"I guess we're noobs then."

"Definitely." She turned toward me. "So, would *you* be freaked out if I *did* have a crush on Shay?"

My little girl did not just ask me that.

Clearly, we were still on that topic.

With a sigh, I thought about how hard Shay hung on every word Kat dropped and couldn't deny they'd make a great couple. He was the calm to her storm, but whenever he could get bogged down with his grand plans, she'd be there to put a smile on his face.

But *still*.

She was my little girl!

"I wouldn't be freaked out," I offered cautiously, "but I wouldn't want you to act on it yet."

"Is this like in the movies? Where I'm not allowed to date anyone until I'm thirty?"

Yes.

Snickering, I grabbed a wooden spoon from the drawer. "No. Though you're not technically allowed to do that anyway, and honestly, you should be grateful. Your mom said thirty-five. I got her down to thirty."

Kat rolled her eyes so hard, I was surprised she didn't fall on her ass. "So, when can I talk to Shay about this?"

"When you're eighteen."

"That's years away!"

"That's how time works."

"But he could be dating someone by then. Victoria, maybe. They're always together," she whined.

"Victoria is a close friend of his." I tapped her nose. "You know that. Plus, she's married."

"Shay's prettier. *He'll* be married by the time I'm that old. This conversation is ruining my life!"

Ah, to be this young.

"Well, you just made me feel ancient. Thank you for that. And here I am, helping you bake!"

Her cheeks gusted out. "Why eighteen?"

"Well, older would be better because of your prefrontal cortex, but also because you're still a kid to him, honey. He loves you. I know that. But you just need to grow up a little bit. Anyway, are you ready for boys? Do you want to kiss them?"

"I want to kiss Shay."

My lips twitched at her mulish expression. "No, you don't."

"I want to hold his hand."

Thank God it was only his hand!

"Well, boys his age, they do a lot more than that. Not that you should let them. You shouldn't. You should do stuff like that when you're ready and never allow anyone to pressure you into anything you don't want to do."

"Including you and Mom when you tell me to clean up the mess I made tonight?"

I grinned. "Nah, kiddo, that's the kind of thing you *have* to listen to. Nice try."

"No fair!"

"Definitely not. *But* it's character building. Or so they say."

"Is this Freud's idea too?"

"Maybe. He came up with some whacko notions."

"He sure did." I almost gagged when she wrote "Shay" in the flour dusting the counter but didn't hide my grimace as she drew a bunch of hearts around his name too. "Do boys do that, then?"

"Do what?"

"Make girls do stuff they don't want to?"

I often came face-to-face with how great a job Star had done on this kid. With her fucked-up background, Star had had her work cut out for her. Like always, she'd knocked it out of the freakin' park.

"They do. And you don't let them. If anyone ever tries, you tell your mom or me and we'll sort it out." I prodded the wooden spoon in the air. "We don't care if you were doing something we told you not to. If the circumstances will get you grounded. You tell us if anyone pressures you to do anything and we'll fix it.

"We can't fix what we don't know, and I'd prefer for you to come to either one of us first. There'll be stuff you'll want to do as you get older. Sneak out of the apartment to go to a club or some other dumb stunt, and it'll put you in danger—that's why if you asked us, we'd say no. But we're not totally ancient. We understand that some things are a rite of passage... not that your mother would like you to believe that.

"Don't let sneaking out stop you from standing your ground *or* from coming to us if you're in trouble. You will always be safe with us. Understood?"

Pursing her lips, she nodded. "And I won't be grounded?"

I knew I was making trouble for future Conor here... "No. Your safety is *all* that matters to us."

That earned me another nod. "Dad?"

"Yes."

"You know I love you, right?"

I shot her a shy smile. "I do. You know I love you too, yeah?"

"When you say stuff like that, I do."

"Good."

"Dad?"

"Yes?"

If my voice sounded wary, that was experience talking. I knew Star had gone through the birds and the goddamn bees a few times, and Kat had even asked questions when I was around, but fuck if I didn't brace myself for a more in-depth convo tonight too.

"Will you help me with a school project?"

My shoulders sagged with relief. "Sure!"

She gnawed on the inside of her cheek. "It's... I don't want Mom to know about it."

"Okay, fine. What is it?"

"We have to make a family tree as an end-of-year project. Shay and I have been working on it, but we hit a wall."

I blew out a breath.

Somehow, I'd have preferred the birds and the bees talk.

"I can tell from your expression you don't mean the O'Donnellys."

She shook her head. "Not just them."

"What do you mean?"

"I want yours, Mom's, and... mine and Alessa's." She peeped at me. "I want to know more about them."

"Are you sure? You might not like what you find out," I warned gently.

"Forewarned is forearmed. Star says that all the time."

"She does." Damn, my wonderful woman. "So, this is you doing that?"

Kat nodded.

I stopped binding the sugar cookie dough together and held out my hand. "We'll work on it together."

She squeezed my fingers. "We won't tell Mom?"

"Well, I will because forewarned *is* forearmed," I said dryly, "and you know we don't keep secrets from each other intentionally. But I'll ask her not to bring it up with you if you don't want her to."

In a tiny voice, she whispered, "I don't want her to."

I rubbed her shoulder. "I understand, cupcake."

When she tunneled her arms around my waist, my lips quirked into a smile and I gently hugged her back.

"What the fuck happened to my kitchen?!"

Both of us jumped at Star's shriek, but ever the little shit, her nose still buried in my sweater, Kat chimed in, "That's ten bucks, please, Mom!"

TEXT CHAT

Camille: I'm so proud of you, @Inessa

Inessa: For dinner?

Camille: YES

Savannah: Honestly, Nessie, well done. I'm proud as well

Aela: Me too

Star: Me three!! That was sheer poetry in motion. Oscar Wilde couldn't have done better himself

Inessa: I didn't do anything. It was all Eoghan, lol

Aoife: What happened?! What are you talking about?

Star: Dinner with the bat out of hell

Aoife: *snorts*

Aoife: Didn't go well?

Star: Oh, no, it was hilarious

Savannah: Lena decided that it was time for Inessa and Eoghan to procreate and that Inessa FAILED Eoghan by not repopulating Manhattan

Aoife: 😨 You have to be kidding me?! Holy shit, Inessa, are you okay?!

Savannah: Of course she is

Star: She has Eoghan LOL

Aoife: He defended you?

Star: HE IMPRESSED me, AOIFE

Star: You know how hard that is

Camille: We're all impressed

Inessa: He didn't even shout

Savannah: Yeah, he definitely learned that skill from my man

Inessa: 🙄

Savannah: What?! It's true! Silent but deadly

Star: Isn't that what we called your pregnancy farts, Vana?

Savannah: STAR! SHUT THE FUCK UP. I did NOT FART

Star: Ohhhhh, right.

Camille: *snickers*

Aela: I definitely heard farting

Inessa: Do we have to talk about this? I have a husband to reward 😈

Star: Yes!!! Go!! You must reward the hero!

Aoife: Holy hell, it was that good?!

Aela: Yeah, it was. Sheeesh. Lena's eyes grew so wide, they were like saucers

Savannah: YOU HELPED MY FATHER CHOOSE MY BRIDE BUT I WON'T LET YOU DEFINE OUR LIVES

Aoife:

Aela: HOW DARE YOU THINK YOU CAN SHAME HER INTO MOTHERHOOD? ANY CHILDREN WE HAVE WILL BE WANTED. NOT FORCED UPON HER LIKE SHE'S A BROODMARE

Aoife: ‼

Camille: My favorite part was: INESSA WILL BE AN AWESOME MOTHER WHEN SHE CHOOSES TO BE ONE. RIGHT NOW, SHE'S FURTHERING HER EDUCATION. SHE'S MAKING SOMETHING OF HERSELF. IF SHE WANTS TO BE A HOMEMAKER, SHE CAN BE, BUT SHE'LL HAVE OPTIONS. I REFUSE TO CULTIVATE THE BELIEF THAT ME AND OUR APARTMENT ARE THE CENTER OF HER WORLD

Aoife: Oh, wow

Camille: Honestly, it was really sweet

Aela: Definitely. SO sweet. He truly meant it

Aoife: I guess that defined the meal?

Aela: Yeah. Things wrapped up after that.

Savannah: The best part was Inessa basically cleared her throat, and all demure-like, murmured, "Eoghan. Enough." And he just shut up.

Star: Very impressive.

Star: 🏆 for him

Savannah: Totally deserved.

Aela: Lena was out of order

Aoife: She probably meant well

Star: Don't defend her! We all have kids and Inessa was one until very recently. They have plenty of time to fill Hell's Kitchen with sprogs if they want to.

Aoife: You're right

Camille: You forgive Lena for too much, Aoife.

Aoife: Hardly!

Savannah: Camille's right. I get it. You were close for a long time but she should have kept her trap shut tonight

Aoife: Agreed. None of her business

Aoife: I didn't mean anything by it. I just, well, I know how her brain works. Eoghan's so up in the air and it's possible she thinks kids will help ground him

Savannah: Without taking into consideration that the O'Donnelly sperm is hazardous waste and they create demon children?

Aela: Hahahaha. I dunno, that shit with the turkey baster was fucking fire.

Savannah: Maybe for you! That was the only time tonight I felt sorry for Lena!

Camille: She'll be walking funny for sure lol

Aoife: Explain?!

Savannah: One word: THIRD

Aoife: Ohhh. You can tell me more tomorrow

Aoife: You guys are still coming into the bakery, right?

Star: Damn straight. I need my fix, PLUS we need to talk about our plan.

Savannah: Aidan already knows how I feel about AI.

Savannah: If you figure out a way to use it on Shay's behalf and make him look good for the presidency, that stealing, pilfering, low-life, scum-sucking piece of walking-copyright-theft tech won't stand a chance

Aela: Tell us how you really feel, Savannah

Savannah: Oh, I will 💯

Aoife: O'Donnellys assemble?

Star: Bahahahaha

FOURTEEN

WHEN AELA SHIMMIED AGAINST ME, my morning wood appreciated the greeting.

Groaning, I pressed my hand to her belly to hold her in place. "Don't tease. Too early for that. What day is it again?"

"24th."

When I grumbled into the back of her neck, she snorted but shimmied again.

"Take the hint, O'Donnelly."

My eyes popped open. "Huh?"

"The hint!" *Another shimmy.*

"Ohhh."

Suddenly wide awake, I slipped my hand down her stomach and realized she'd worn one of those baggy shirts to bed.

How hadn't I noticed that the night before? Not that I was complaining—easy access, for the fucking win.

I groaned again. "No panties?!"

"None."

Her breathless tone had me nipping her shoulder. "Why didn't you tell me last night?"

"Because I wanted to sleep. Now, I'd very much like for my husband to fuck me before I have to go and make breakfast."

"Your husband can definitely help with that. And breakfast too."

She moaned. "That might be the sexiest thing you've said this month."

"Then I need to work on my dirty talk." I let my tongue flutter over to her pulse point as my hand slipped between her thighs.

Levering her leg, she hooked it over my knee, and I hissed when I found her warmth. Just on the brink of wetness. And from her "squirmy" state, I knew she'd been reading on her phone before she'd woken me up.

"What was it?" I breathed in her ear before nipping the lobe. "One of Aoife and Inessa's recommendations?"

"Yessss."

She shuddered as I fingered her clit then reached for the hem of her sleep shirt and dragged it up to her chest. When her fingers plucked at her nipple, I muttered, "I can't see shit in here. Fucking daylight savings—"

"Use your imagination. Don't stop!" The hitch in her breath had me nipping her throat. "Ugh, you're going to leave a hickey."

"Is that a complaint?"

"No, but we're too old for hickeys."

"Ha!" I nipped her again. For extra measure. "Never too old." I licked where I'd attacked and sucked, pressing down hard until she bucked back into me.

Veering away from her clit, I quickly slid my fingers down and tested her readiness.

"So wet for me, baby."

"God, I hate you when you leave love bites, but they feel so good," she mewled.

"That's because I give you what you want. You're just too shy to ask."

Though she chuckled, it died off midway through. "Fuck, Dec. That's it. Grind your—"

I pressed the heel of my hand against her clit and let her work herself over. "You are so fucking hot, Aela. I love how wet you get for me. Nothing better in this world than waking up with you in my arms like this."

Her tight pussy clung to my knuckles.

"Go on, baby. Use me. Get yourself off. You earned it. By being so fucking awesome. My god, you amaze me." Her cunt fluttered in reaction to my words. "Just feel that. So hot and wet. So tight. I can't wait to slide my cock into you. I'm going to goddamn explode once I sink home.

"But you're gonna be even tighter because you're not getting my dick until you come. Hear that, baby? Now, be a good girl for me and just let yourself feel."

My crooned words had her breath hitching again as I toyed with her pussy, giving it to her exactly how she loved.

And like the good girl she could sometimes be, she obeyed and took her pleasure. Focused on it and released the softest of keening cries as it shattered through her.

"So goddamn hot. Well, how's that feel, Aela? My wife. *Mine.*" I continued thrusting, but gently now. When she shuddered in my arms, I rasped, "So wet and warm. God, you really are fucking perfect. I think I know that and then I touch you again and it just reminds me of how little I know and how much there is for me to remember, until it's cleaved in my memory for-fucking-ever."

"Dec," she warbled, her lower body tensing. "I need your cock. Please. Fuck me."

"Whatever my wife needs, she gets."

I let my fingers retreat but gave her clit a gentle pat that had her gasping.

Pulling my cock free from my boxer briefs, I slipped it between her thighs. Then, I covered her sex with my hand and tipped her hips back.

"You gonna put me inside you, baby?"

"Goddammit, Dec," she mewled.

My laughter was gritty in her ear, but it morphed into a growl as her fingers, those clever, wicked fingers stroked over my length. She didn't mess around or tease. Whatever dirty scene she'd read in her book, I had to thank the author for because holy fuck, she wanted hers this morning.

One second, I was out in the cold.

The next, my dick sheathed itself inside her.

Slowly, I pushed into her because she was still tight as fuck thanks to her recent orgasm, but so goddamn juicy that I slipped in just right.

"Declan," she whimpered, turning her head into the pillow, but I tutted and slipped my hand higher, cupping her throat to encourage her to tilt her face toward me.

"No hiding," I chided as I nibbled on her bottom lip, then swiped my tongue over it. "You like my cock in you, baby?"

"God, yes. You feel so good. Thank you."

"For?"

"Getting a vasectomy," she rasped, making me snort.

"You like it when I come in you, huh? Maybe I should make you walk around with me inside you all morning," I rumbled. "Just a little reminder who owns this pussy."

She shuddered. "You know you do."

"You sure you haven't forgotten? Maybe those heroes in those books are looking hot to you," I teased, because only a weak-minded, lazy asshole could be jealous of a fictional character.

Who was I to complain if words got my wife hot? I was the lucky chump who reaped the rewards.

I tipped my goddamn hat to smut authors everywhere.

"Not as hot as you."

"You sure? Your fingers didn't hit the spot like mine?"

She tensed. "Huh?"

"Your pussy was a little too juicy." I nipped her earlobe again. "You tried to get off without giving me a show. You know my cock's yours to use."

"Is it?" Aela sagged. "Whenever I need it?"

"Fuck, yeah. When you need me inside you, I'm there." I pressed a kiss to her lips. "Just use me, baby. Whenever you want."

"Oh, god." As she whimpered, her cunt clamped down on me. "Fuck me, Dec. Please. God, I need you to move—"

I might not be book smart, but I was a genius in "Aela." She practically fucked me from below as she wriggled and writhed, the idea of using me like that clearly an epic turn-on.

I pumped my dick into her, giving her what she needed. Her imagination did half the job, and when she came, she released a hiss. "Don't stop. Please, don't ever stop, Dec."

"I won't," I vowed. "I won't. But I'm close, baby. So fucking close. Your pussy is perfect. You cling to me just right. How the hell am I not supposed to come?"

"Oh," she whined as I carried her straight on through that one.

"Can you get another? Show me how you touched your pussy earlier."

With an immediacy that had me laughing, she grabbed my hand and directed me. All the while, I thrust into her, not lazily but not frenzied either. If I did, then I'd come too fast.

I focused on touching her, on reminding her why she was mine, and I felt the sweetest burst inside her as she melted around me. Her whole body fell limp as she shuddered through it, releasing the softest of sweet sighs and the cutest, "Oh!"

As her pussy clutched at me, I breathed in her ear, "Baby?"

She hummed. All sleepy and relaxed and cum-tired. "I want you to come inside me, Declan. I want to feel you. I need you. I always need you. Please, give me your cum."

I sped up. "You sure you want it?"

"I do." She bridged our fingers together, then tightened her knuckles around mine. "I always need it. Always want you."

"Always? You sure?"

She growled. "Stop teasing me!"

I growled back in her ear, "So feisty."

"We can do a science experiment next time and you can figure it out for yourself, but if you don't give me your cum right now, I'll scream!"

"And I'd have a problem with that because…?"

Her snarl had me shuddering, especially as she bucked her hips into me.

"Fuck, you fill me so good *when you stop teasing me.*" Her moan morphed into a desperate whimper. "Please, Dec. Give it to me. I need—"

My heart stilled as I allowed myself to come. It flowed through me, the sharpest of heats as I exploded inside her, hips jerking while I rode the wave. Short and disjointed thrusts that had her releasing breathy sighs.

When I sagged next to her, my own breaths were heavy with exertion.

"Jesus."

I blinked, enjoying her soft, lighthearted chuckle.

"Nah, Aela. That's my name."

I bit her shoulder. Just because. "You sure?"

"Definitely." She snickered then turned her face toward me. "That was perfect."

"Yeah. It was. Jesus."

"Aela."

Chortling in her ear, I squirreled my arm under her waist and hugged her from behind. "Wanna nap?"

"No. We have stuff to do before we head to the cemetery today."

Shit. "I hate going there."

"I know, but it's tradition."

"Fucking tradition."

"Your ma won't be happy if you tell her you didn't go," she said slyly.

"It should be illegal to talk about that while my cock's still inside you."

"You're the lawbreaker, not me. *You'd* know."

"Then I'm making it a law."

"You can. But you're still going today. At least your ma left yesterday and we won't have to watch her break down."

I hid my face in her throat because yeah, that was always hard to witness. "Hate it. So many fucked-up memories."

She wiggled when my dick slipped free. "I know, baby. But I don't want to lie in the wet spot so let me get up."

"Party pooper," I joked before I spun her around and yanked her into my arms.

She yelped but locked her hands behind my head. "My hero."

I snorted when she batted her lashes. "I try."

I hit the night light I'd had installed because I fucking hated pissing at four AM with a light bright enough to perform surgery and trudged over to the bathtub.

"I don't have time for a bath."

"We'll make time," I chided, lowering her gently to the side. "Hey, did you get the matching PJs for tonight?"

"Thought you hated that tradition."

I'd deny, in a court of fucking law, that my cheeks pinkened. "Cam likes it."

"Ah, Cam, huh?"

I ignored her chuckle. "Well? Did you?"

"Maybe that should be your chore next year, seeing as it's so important to you and *Cam*."

"Where the fuck do you buy stuff like that?"

"A store, Declan. A store. It's a place where they have things for sale and you can go and purchase them. Your brother's wife will probably have a home collection next year—"

"Which one?"

"Dec!"

I hid a grin. "What?!"

"You'd better be joking right now."

"About?"

"Jesus Christ, don't tell me you've sat through strategy meetings and—" Her eyes narrowed. "You *are* joking."

"Of course I am. Haven't heard anything about a home store. Where they sell towels and shit? Should I rec that to Finn?"

"Probably. It'd work too. Do some influencer collabs and Eef's set."

"You should talk to Finn about that."

"Mid-Christmas movie or dinner?" she taunted, but she finally turned on the faucets and fiddled with the water temperature.

"Finn won't mind."

"I'll mind! I'm not talking world domination over turkey. Certainly not Aoife's turkey."

"You're right. I think she laces it with fairy dust or something. That shit's never dry." I rubbed my chin as I faced the mirror, where a couple days' worth of scruff awaited me.

"Your ma's reaction to you not shaving was priceless."

"She asked me if I was taking lessons from Uncle Paddy," I said around a grin. "I told her she needed to take lessons from Aoife on the stuffing front."

"You didn't!"

"I did. She asked me why I hadn't cleared my plate. After the Uncle Paddy comment, I wasn't going to hold back."

The pseudo-Christmas meal at Ma's had been great—for the most part. Until Ma had turned psycho on Inessa not having given Eoghan any kids yet.

Honestly, it was a relief Ma had gone out of town. Only Inessa threatening Eoghan had gotten him to stop laying into Ma, and I fully intended on enjoying the holidays.

Having an older kid, I knew we were lucky to still have Shay around for Christmas.

There'd come a time when he'd prefer to be with his buds or his girlfriend's family.

The only reason we barely saw Aela's was because she preferred my batshit parent to her own.

So I'd hug this potential last holiday with my son to my chest.

Your daughter's your daughter for life. But your son's your son until he gets a wife...

I arched a brow at Aela when I realized she'd said something I'd missed.

"What, babe?"

"You should grow a beard."

I chuckled. "Nah."

"Why not? You hate shaving."

I peered at her over my shoulder. "You go pink when I don't shave. Not putting your skin through that. I only didn't yesterday because Cameron set off the fire alarm and distracted me. And the day before..."

Well, I wasn't bringing Victoria's situation up by choice.

Thankfully, Cam's shenanigans distracted her.

"He did what?!"

"It was fine." It wasn't. I still didn't know how he'd set the fucker off either.

"How was it fine? What did he do?"

"I don't know."

"That's why you replaced it yesterday?"

I shrugged.

"You know it's not snitching when you're the dad, right?"

"Of course." I still rubbed my chin. "He's going to be a nightmare. I can already see it."

"Don't sound so delighted."

"It'll be fun!"

"It'll be something."

"Shay never got into that much trouble, did he?"

"No." She stared down at the water. "I often wonder if he repressed that side of himself. When I see how much mayhem Jake and Cam cause when they're in a room together and I think about Shay... I thought we were happy."

"Of course you were. It's the O'Donnelly influence. Hellraisers, the lot of us. Ma's insane for a reason. Imagine raising six of us!"

She pursed her lips. "You think?"

"I know." I took a seat beside her on the tub. "What did you tell me? Shay's Shay and Cam's Cam.

"Some souls are always older. I think that's Eoghan for us. Even before he served overseas, he had a way of seeing the world that defied his age." Curving my arm around her shoulder, I rested my head against hers. "But we definitely need to watch Cam around devices that beep."

"Bah! What did he do?"

No way was I admitting I didn't know for real. She thought I was messing with her—I wasn't! And I hadn't been fucking around either —I'd gone to take a goddamn leak!

The last thing a man expected was to use the restroom and for the fire alarm to go off.

I'd end up with PTSD after eighteen years of this.

"I may sic him on Conor. Maybe he's a technological genius who needs his skills honed in." Quickly, I changed the subject. "You got your gift done?"

"You're changing the subject," she accused.

"Did I ever tell you that you're the best, smartest, most gorgeous wife in the world?"

"Funny how I'm always that when you've been watching Cameron and he pulls some Houdini stunt on you."

Crossing my fingers behind my back, I shot her a winning smile. "Father-son bonding time. You can't beat it."

FIFTEEN

IT WAS a toss-up what I hated more about Christmas Eve.

Visiting Da's grave—no matter the weather.

Mass—boring.

The kids' play at church—funny, but I only liked seeing my nieces and nephews on stage.

The movie we had to watch together—*The Nightmare Before Christmas.*

Having an eidetic memory made the latter torture, the play a sensory hell, and mass a nightmare. Thank fuck we were home.

With a relieved sigh, I dropped onto my seat, growling when Katina's cats began weaving in and out of my legs.

To stop them, I crossed my ankles and then rolled my eyes when they curled up beside me. So close, I could feel them breathing.

At first, their mismatched heartbeats had a nerve twitching in my left eye but, once I adapted, the sensations soothed me.

When I'd settled, everyone else scrambled for their positions, but the rest of these fuckers I called family knew that this was my spot.

You only sat here if you had a death wish.

From here, I could see out of the window, into the hall, over the city, and the surrounding roofs.

Ma and Uncle Paddy might have been overseas, but the bulk of my people were here, safe, *not* sound, and always annoying.

"Stop sighing." Inessa tutted beside me, simultaneously shoving her tit into my arm and dropping the extra-large bowl of popcorn on my lap, the one we both pretended I didn't eat.

Now, *this* was bliss.

Ren hissed at her backtalking to me then gifted Inessa the *coûp de grace*—a butthole-shaped salute before taking off.

As Pebbles jumped up beside Inessa and spun in a circle until she found the perfect spot, I drawled, "I'm not sighing."

"You're sighing."

"Why does Katina always bring these damn cats anyway?"

"You know you love them."

Ha!

The kids, already dressed in Christmas PJs, leaped around like the freaky ass skeleton would be loping around Christmas Town once Star finished setting up a dangling star *piñata*.

"Only she'd pick a star."

Star sniped, "I heard that, fu— ja— I mean, Eoghan. What could I do? The store only had this shape left in stock!"

"Narcissist." I rolled my eyes as she flipped me the bird before carrying on with the task.

"Already told her that," Troy declared. "And it isn't in the middle."

"Everyone's a damn critic," Star snarled. "If you want to center it, *you* do it, Troy."

As the pair started bickering, I told Inessa, "I'm not sure this is a wise decision."

"Troy made the puzzle a tradition, so Star wants this to be hers."

"She has violence in her soul, that one."

"And you don't?"

"Hell, they're never with us anyway on Christmas Eve. They're only here this year because stomach flu swarmed the Sinners' compound."

Inessa gagged. "Gross."

"I hit too. I hit too," Roman shrieked, snagging our attention.

"Like father, like son," I called out, earning me a scowl from Brennan.

"Oh, yeah, Uncle Brennan," Kat yelled from the dining room, loud enough to make me wince. "I told Alessa to tell Nyx that if he comes to the city again, you'll pickle him, but I don't understand the logistics of that. How do you pickle a human being?"

"Pickle!" Third shrieked, earning a proud look from her father.

"No pickles tonight, baby." He kissed her crown. "*Pizza.*"

As Third took off like a bat out of hell, crowing about *pissa*, Brennan hollered back, "Best not to ask questions, Kat. But thank you for passing along the warning."

"I'll pickle *you* later for having my daughter be the go-between," Star sang in a tone that warned of a painful, painful, painful death.

"Says you," Savannah drawled. "You use Kat as a go-between all the time."

"I do not!"

"Sure you do. Alessa still blames you for—"

"Never mind!" Star glared at Savannah, who shrugged.

"Just keeping things fair."

"I'll remember your idea of fairness next time," Star intoned.

"I hit! I hit! I hit!" Roman reminded us, tugging on his mom's arm to get the action going.

Armed with mini baseball bats that the kids wielded with all the promise of being future pro players/great fists for the Firm, I grunted as Jake managed to smash the *piñata* within two tries. Niall and Roman were way too small, but as candy cascaded over the floor, they cackled in glee and let it rain over their heads.

Third shrieked at Declan, who just so happened to be holding her after we collectively agreed never to allow her near weapons. Not when she almost impaled Ma with a turkey baster the other day. Still,

I wasn't surprised when he put her down; she shrieked loud enough to take out an eardrum.

Happy once liberated from imprisonment, Third dashed over to be with her buds—Roman, Niall, and her were thicker than thieves.

Which, again, boded well for the Firm.

It was almost a shame Da couldn't see it for himself. He'd have been proud as fuck.

While LyLy picked up a couple pieces of candy from the floor, ones that weren't being squished by two toddlers with main character energy, Cam hopped on his feet and kept on swinging until Declan, his hands free now, swept in, tilted him upside down, and dangled him.

"Get him, kids!" he cheered as the others—aside from Jake—abandoned the candy to tickle Cam, who yelped and squealed and giggled. Even Benjamim, who was the quietest of Star and Conor's kids.

I'd admit—that earned a smile out of me.

Especially when the cacophony of animals we had all got in on the action—even Pebbles jumped down from her place beside Inessa, and Ren and Stimpy deigned to stop using my feet as pillows to join in.

"Holy cow, was that a smile?" Inessa inquired with a mock-gasp.

"Nah."

She hooted. "Just like you refuse to admit that *Maxton Hall* intrigued you?"

"I was *not* intrigued."

"That's why you were asking questions about it, huh?"

"You read the book!"

"Well? You can read it too."

"Maybe I will."

"Don't threaten me with a good time." She snickered. "I can include you in my reading nook. I'll even share my armchair with you."

Interested in the prospect, I arched a brow. "Seriously? That's the only place I'm not welcome in the apartment."

"You're welcome. You're just not allowed to disturb me."

"I'll think about it."

"You do that," she said smugly then laughed. "Jake's focused on the prize."

"Just like his father. Watch him share it, though. He's a sucker for Cam."

"He's his baby bro. LyLy has them wrapped around her finger too." Finn chuckled. "I think I'm seeing a trend. All the girls are nightmares and the boys are their supporting acts."

Inessa crowed, "Rightly so."

I glanced over at Finn, who smiled at the scene before him. It was hard to believe that he'd get sappy over this shit, but becoming a father was hell on the heart. I'd seen four of my siblings fall into that madness, so I recognized the descent.

"You ever think about how Da must have been before he had kids?"

Finn's brows shot up. "No. I don't willingly give myself nightmares."

"He wouldn't have been *that* bad," Inessa excused as she dipped her hand into the popcorn bowl.

"Says who?" I scoffed.

"Who wouldn't have been that bad?" Brennan asked.

When he tried to get some of Inessa's popcorn, I hissed. "Get your fucking own. This is Inessa's."

Brennan jolted when Ren and Stimpy joined me in hissing at him in my defense.

"Oh, it's like that, is it?"

"Yeah, it fucking is."

Finn heaved a sigh. "If I have to break you two and the crepes apart, I will."

"Camille's methods worked." Inessa chuckled. "I'll even tell you where we store the produce if you need to know."

"Not more potatoes." Brennan groaned, but pride loaded down his grin.

Inessa smirked as I shook my head—that tale had made the rounds at Ma's calamity of a Christmas meal. "If Camille's at the end of her tether, then it's Finn we have to feel sorry for. You've been dealing with this a lot longer than we have."

I lifted my hand and played the world's tiniest violin.

Finn shoved my arm. "They're talking about Da, Brennan. If having kids softened him."

Brennan sneered, "Yeah, I don't think so. Or if it did, it happened by the time you were born, Eoghan. It's why you're such a fucking brat."

I narrowed one eye at him, aimed my finger, and lifted it sharply. "I know where you sleep."

"And your wife is my wife's sister so my ass is fucking safe." Brennan sneered at me and, giving the cats a wide berth, stalked over to the other couch, where he tugged Camille onto his lap like she was his real-life teddy bear.

"You two spend too much time together," Finn remarked.

"I've had him over three nights this week! *And* we'll be having Orthodox celebrations here!"

"Stop grumbling." Inessa jabbed my arm with a fingernail. "We only have it at home because you can ensure the perimeter's secure. He accommodates your issues all the time— *Oh, Jake!* Look at your haul." He shot her a shy smile and handed her a piece of candy. She squealed. "I love this one."

Finn tugged Jake onto his lap. "What you got there, little man? Anything Daddy likes?"

As they divvied up their treasure, Aoife hurried along with three pizza boxes stacked in her arms. Conor, Aela, and Declan came with three apiece too.

When they set the boxes on the coffee table, I peered at them and heaved a sigh.

If pizza had arrived, then that meant the movie was about to begin.

"You can always go and help with the puzzle if this is so bad," Finn joked.

Puzzle, *piñata,* and pizza.

Jesus H. Christ.

I ignored his smirk and accepted the eggnog that Aela passed me with a muttered, "Thanks."

"Don't thank me. Inessa made it."

"It's good," Finn praised.

"I made it in October!"

"After three tries," I whispered in her ear, laughing when she whacked my thigh. "Wonder if Aidan's too bougie to drink it. You know he prefers his million-dollar bottles of hooch."

"Hey! Leave my man alone. We all need a hobby," Savannah cried.

Curving his arm around her, Aidan smirked. "What can I say? I'm a man with great taste."

"Damn straight!"

"What are you doing here again?" Inessa drawled.

Savannah stuck out her tongue.

Normally, Aidan, Savvie, and Third went to the Daniels' for the 24th. But this year, Dagger was on his farewell tour before retiring.

Allegedly.

He'd already retired four times. But he and Camden were doing a special gig or something. The farewell to end all farewells.

I snagged one of the paper plates Aoife had dropped on the coffee table before taking a seat beside Finn and Jake.

Picking up a couple slices, I watched as Aidan commandeered my TV and set up the movie.

I sometimes wondered how we'd reached this space in our lives where we watched kids movies and ate pizza and had built-in traditions that meant I could never escape my fucking family for more than two minutes over the holidays.

Then I'd stop thinking about it because living it was bad enough.

When that weird fucking skeleton darted around Christmas Town like Jake on too many Skittles, I muttered, "Why is it always this movie?"

"Tradition."

I tipped my head back. "I hate tradition."

"You love it."

"I hate it.'

"You love it. You like being around your family—"

Ha!

"At their places!"

"You're the one who insists they come here." Her lips curved when I grunted. "The truth hurts, Grinch."

"I'm not green."

"That's the only argument you have?"

"My heart doesn't grow."

"So you know the story."

I sniffed. "I overheard Finn reading it to Jake one year."

"Your heart grows."

"Nah."

"Grew for me. And other parts of you triple in size when I'm around."

I chortled. "You're not wrong, babe."

"Anyway, not long until *Die Hard* starts."

"It *is* a Christmas movie."

"If you say so," she sang, then glanced over her shoulder when the puzzle they were working on triggered an argument between Kat and Shay. All while Kat intermittently conspired with Troy. *The true nightmare before Christmas.* "Star told me Kat's been on edge since she and Conor began looking into her family history."

"Is that the project we're not allowed to talk about?"

"Yup."

"So why are we talking about it?"

She clucked her tongue. "Man, you really did wake up on the wrong side of the bed this morning."

"I think you'll find I woke up on the right side of the bed because you were on my side and I was inside *you*. Plus, our apartment was empty."

Color burnished her cheeks and she hastened to change the direction of our conversation: "Are you sure Victoria's okay? It doesn't feel right, her not being here."

I patted her arm. "She's fine. She said she'd be with us tomorrow."

Finn, with his gaze locked on the screen, casually commented, "If you need some space, I'll cover for you."

Because that was our cue, I rumbled, "Yeah. I'll just grab some snacks. Thanks, bro," and slid out from the sofa and slunk over to the kitchen and then into my bedroom.

I didn't have long because she was my radar and that meant she'd find me out. She always did. Even when I flipped back on myself and used goddamn skills that had cost multiple governments millions of dollars in training—Inessa knew where I was. *Without Conor's help.*

For one night only, I wouldn't begrudge that skill and would be grateful for it.

Pulling open the bottom drawer in my dresser in our walk-in closet, I retrieved the box and I hustled into our bedroom.

"In the future, don't make plans on Christmas Eve because they turn you into a gnarly fucker," I chided myself as I shifted ass around the bedroom, well aware that time ticked down.

I made it—barely.

When soft footsteps padded through this section of the apartment, I flicked off the switch and let darkness and the city's ghostly lights illuminate the space.

Then, I waited.

The door popped open and I saw her peer through the gap. Even saw her surprise when darkness faced her.

"Eoghan?!" she demanded, pushing the door wider. "Where the

hell are you? What does Finn need to cover for you?" She flicked the switch then jumped when she noticed me. "What are you doing?!"

I shot her a winsome smile. "What do you think?"

She blinked a few times. "You're surrounded by rose petals and are on one knee. But I'm offended you don't remember the whole 'us at the church' thing." Still, her smile lit up her eyes as she slipped deeper into the bedroom, clearly curious, after closing the door behind her.

"Oh, I remember. And I remember how I was a jerk before—"

"You're always a jerk," she dismissed cheerily. "It's kinda nice you being down there. I don't have to strain my neck. Well? What's going on?"

I proffered the small box to her. "You're my wife, Inessa. You put up with too much of my bullshit—"

"You're not supposed to swear when you're proposing!" she reprimanded, but she laughed as she accepted the box without opening it. "Carry on!"

"You put up with my moods and my stalking and my incessant need to protect you, and I never really expected this Russian brat my da tied me to to be any of those things. I thought you'd be the millstone around my neck—"

"Charming!"

"Instead, I'm that for you."

Her lips rounded and any amusement wiped from her expression. "You take that back!"

I jolted in surprise at her hissed demand. "What?"

"Take it back. Eoghan, you are not a millstone around my neck. You accept me. Don't you see that? My god, you give me freedom when it pains you to do so, but you still do it. I have so much more freedom than I ever expected to have.

"I go to college and you let my sister meddle in our lives and her home is our second house because we spend so much time together— I never expected to have that. You gave me a safe enough space to bring her around. Never mind Victoria.

"If you were anyone else, I don't know what would have happened to her because fuck, I couldn't trust anyone in my father's world with her." She straightened her shoulders. "But fuck safety. You make me happy!

"You brought me this crazy family that drives me insane and has all these traditions. You never do what I think you will and are apparently going to buddy up with me in my reading nook. You consider me. All the time. Always.

"I'd have borne a battalion of *heirs* and daughters to marry off to allies by now if you were anyone else. With barely any time in between if you were anything like my father and kept on popping out girls. No freedom, no education, no bodily autonomy, no partnership, no *joy*.

"You are such a wonderful husband, Eoghan. Don't you dare say otherwise in my presence."

A shocked laugh escaped me. But my lips curved in surprised pleasure. "I know I have issues."

"And I don't? We get through them together and we'll carry on doing that." She shoved the box back at me. "I don't want this, whatever it is, if you're questioning the years we've spent together and are thinking I want to rewrite any of it."

My Adam's apple bobbed when she took a step backward. I surged upward, snagged her in my arms, and held her as close as I could, tucking her face into my chest with my hand cupping the back of her head. All while I rested my chin on her shoulder, encompassing her in me.

"That isn't what this is about," I rasped.

"Then what is?"

"You never got this."

"Got what?"

"The 'me on my knee' thing."

She paused, then released the softest, happiest of laughs. "You're mad and I'm here for it, don't get me wrong, but I didn't need this, Eoghan."

"All your damn books have these moments!"

"Not all of them." She wrestled free of my embrace so she could stare back at me. "And they don't tend to happen in a married couple's bedroom, though the roses are a nice touch."

My nose scrunched. "Well, I know you like the family around, but no way in hell was I going to do this in front of them—"

"This is your idea of a compromise, huh?"

"Exactly." My expression softened. "You make me happy, Inessa. All I want is to make you feel the same."

Her eyes widened. "You do, Eoghan. Every day." Then, quick as lightning, she grinned at me as she pressed another soft kiss to my lips. "I have to tell you something."

I immediately stiffened. "What?"

"I didn't want to say... not yet. It's close to the safe period."

My tone sharpened with urgency, but I couldn't dampen it. "What?!"

"I'm pregnant."

The soft smile that curved her lips stole my breath, never mind her words. I stared at her. The glow. The gleam. *The fucking joy.*

I literally existed in her happiness.

My arms tightened around her. "I want to be there for all the appointments."

"No way! You'll have a gun to the doctor's head—" She broke off. "If you don't, you'll be watching from a rooftop, won't you?"

"Gun trained on the *back* of that fucker's head."

"Eoghan," she whined, but her smile was gleeful. "You're a nut."

"My nut's in you."

"I refuse to call our baby 'Nut.'"

My throat bobbed. "How about... *Bump?*"

She pulled back ever so slightly and grabbed my hands to rest them on her stomach. "No bump. Yet."

"Yet."

That effervescent smile made another appearance. "Yet."

"I'm glad you didn't tell Ma."

She smirked, her angelic features darkening. "Holding my tongue was hard, but I refused for that to be the place I told you our family was growing."

Passing her the box, I smoothed my fingers over the still-slim expanse of her abdomen. "Thank you, sweetheart."

"You're welcome."

"Okay, so, now I think my Christmas gift sucks."

"Doubtful."

Unsure, I hitched a shoulder. "Open the box."

She pulled back and slipped it open, not complaining when I kept a hold of her waist.

Her brows lifted when she came across a QR code on a piece of paper. Not a ring.

"Do you have your phone?"

"Of course I do," she scoffed, slipping it from one of those magical spots on her person where she'd tucked it away in an outfit free from pockets.

She scanned the QR code and frowned at the image that popped up. "What is this?"

But I just shrugged, still trying to discern the faintest of changes in her. I'd be goddamn checking her out later, mapping every difference until I knew her body better than she did.

Utterly unaware of my intentions, her eyes narrowed as she increased her screen's brightness and zoomed in on the picture where the damn elf sat that Finn had insisted was a good idea.

It taunted her with a cheery smile and a wave.

She wiggled her head from side to side as she tried to figure out the elf's location, then stormed off, uncaring that she dislodged my hands.

Because they couldn't hold her, I shoved them in my pockets and traipsed behind her, a wider smile curving my lips.

Here was me, thinking I still had it in me to keep her on her toes...

Inessa: 1

Eoghan: 0

SIXTEEN

IT TOOK ten minutes for the kids to realize that Inessa wasn't focused on the movie and that Eoghan was following her around the apartment.

Of course, that meant they had to follow him too.

Eoghan fascinated them. Maybe it was because he made no real effort with them. In that way of ornery kids, and my brothers only produced ornery spawn, that intrigued them all the more.

Why hang around the people who actually wanted you there when you could irritate the one who didn't?

Kat trundled after her next. Then, ever nosy, Third waddled along, tugging at Kat in a silent demand to be carried.

That kid was her mother's daughter. Why walk when other people's arms existed to do the work for her?

Aoife was the first adult to follow, sheer curiosity getting her to abandon the movie ten minutes from the end.

The sly smile on my wife's face told me she knew exactly what was happening.

Inessa was hard to ignore—she didn't care if she walked in front of the screen in her haste to find whatever she saw on her phone.

The first time, she ended up dragging out some books from under the TV and shouted, "A-ha!"

"What is it, Aunty Nessie?" Jake asked, peering around her shoulder.

Soft eyes found my youngest brother. "It's a signed book I wanted."

Cam, never one to be excluded when Jake was in on something, prodded her. "There's a QR thingy, Auntie Nessie."

"Oh! So there is."

She scanned it, and off she went again.

Another signed book. Orient Express tickets from Istanbul to Venice. Emerald earrings the size of my thumbnails.

With each gift, my brothers—apart from Finn—all grew dramatically grimmer.

"That asshole's showing us up!"

Camille snorted at Declan's outrage. "How is he showing you up?"

"I bought Aela a cottage in fucking Poughkeepsie because Shay's at Oakwood College and that's not impressive now!"

Aidan scratched his jaw. "I got Savvie a set of Da's journals I salvaged. You don't even want to know what I had to do to make Ma let go of them."

Camille clucked her tongue. "Aidan, that's perfect for Savannah. You know she'll want to write his biography...?"

"I know." He grimaced when we all glowered at him. "I figured we'd work out later how to talk her down."

"Jesus, Aidan!" Finn sighed.

"Maybe she could write it as a fictional book?" Camille offered, ever helpful.

I had a fucking saint as a wife.

My hand tightened around hers and I lifted her knuckles to my lips to kiss them.

"I got Aoife a new kitchen," Finn demurred.

"Like you didn't know what Eoghan was up to," I mocked. "I saw you giving him eye signals."

"I helped put the gifts where he told me to. That was my only input."

"Yeah, right," Aidan jeered.

"Aoife wanted a new kitchen, Finn." Camille tsked. "So she'll love your gift. What about you, Conor?"

"Star liked the early gift I made her—"

"Don't ask questions." Aidan took a deep sip of whiskey. "If he made it, then it's bound to be fucking weird."

"Hey!" Conor pouted. "I resent that. I single-handedly brought orgasms to orgasmless women according to her."

Camille's brows lifted. "What?!"

"Well, it wasn't for women the world over," he admitted. "Just her, but she seemed to like it. Oh, and I'm a few months away from having enough details on Justice Brackenreid to blackmail him."

Conor and his hobby of bending the Supreme Court to his—read Star's—*will.*

"I'm sure that'll make her very happy."

"Oh, definitely," Conor chirped. "What does she have now?"

Camille smiled as Inessa curved her arms around Eoghan's neck and hauled him close. "Is that the lodge, Finn?"

"Yeah, she has a key in her hand."

"Lodge?" I queried.

"A compromise. Inessa hates camping," she joked.

"Ah."

"You once told me this place would be your gilded cage," Eoghan rasped, loud enough for most of the people in the room to hear. "But you'll never be caged. Not as long as I'm alive."

I heaved a sigh when he kissed her and Camille awwwwed.

The rest of my brothers and I shared another stern look that promised we'd be beating the fuck out of Eoghan as soon as the holidays were over.

Little shit never stopped over-fucking-achieving.

On the cusp of midnight, Inessa had a new Aston Martin and popped open a ring box with an engagement ring that, by the sounds of it, Camille had helped him pick.

Aidan, in self-defense, put *Die Hard* on, and I let Camille go hang out with the girls, who were all cooing over Inessa's gifts.

"Fucker's making us look bad," Declan repeated.

Finn shook his head. "Our gifts are good enough."

"There's good enough and then there's this!"

"I thought you got Aela that painting she liked on top of the cottage?"

He frowned at me. "I did. But that's not *this!* Talk about a fucking love letter to her."

"More like treasure map," Conor teased. "Declan, they'll love what we got them."

"You never said what your gift is," Aidan prodded.

"I wasn't going to say it in front of her, dipshit," I dismissed.

"Well, she's over there cooing with—" Aidan broke off and glared at Eoghan. "Oi, fucker. What was this about?"

Eoghan slunk into the only seat he'd use on this damn sofa which, of course, was across the damn room from us so we all had to move over there.

He shrugged. "Don't know what you're talking about."

Declan punched his shoulder. "You asshole."

A low-level smirk danced on Eoghan's face. "I can't help it if I'm the romantic one of us."

"The romantic one?!" Conor squawked. "Fuck you!"

Eoghan eyed Conor. "Don't make out as if your gift to Star won't be perfect for her." His gimlet stare skewered each of us as he growled, "You picked your brides and they picked you. Inessa and I didn't get that. I was rectifying the past."

He didn't have that exactly right. My beginnings with Camille had been fraught with their own stressors—not that they knew that. Not really.

"So you're not going to show us up next year?" Finn teased, because he seemed the least worried of all of us.

Eoghan shrugged, but I answered, "He set himself up for a fall. He has to beat this."

When Eoghan grimaced, we cackled.

"Fuck you."

"No, thanks," I joked, settling back in my seat.

But for all the shit I gave him, I knew he was right—Inessa hadn't had a choice, neither had he. With how much time I spent around Inessa and Victoria, I knew they deserved the world.

And if Maxim Lyanov hadn't figured that out yet, Eoghan and I had ways of convincing a man to agree with us.

Three hours later, Camille and I made it to our parking garage.

"Okay, game plan. You grab Roman's stuff and overnight bags and I'll get the gifts?"

After the fam had decided we'd converge on Finn and Aoife's place, as they were hosting tomorrow, for an impromptu sleepover, all the parents had returned to their respective homes to pick up the gifts.

"Well, we *could* do that."

Once I'd pulled into my spot, I arched a brow. "We're heading back to Finn and Aoife's..."

"Yes. *After*."

"You have plans for me, huh?"

"Definitely. Concrete ones." She leaned down to stick her shoes on then whined, "Brennnnnan."

I hid a smirk. "You chose to wear them."

"I wore these for you so you *have* to carry me upstairs."

"Like a piggyback?"

Dumping the heels back in the footwell, she crowed, "That would mean *I'd* be riding *you* and from the back. Sounds like no fun."

"So, what's the new game plan?"

"That we take advantage of an empty apartment while Aoife and Finn are looking after our baby?"

"Sounds like you're smarter than me."

Before I shut off the engine, she hit the button that moved my seat back. When she scuttled over onto my lap, I sighed as I set my hands on her hips.

I smoothed one hand over the length of her spine. "Thought your feet ached."

"You can rub them later."

"Last time we did this, you got cramps."

She looped her arms around my neck. "Brennan O'Donnelly! Are you trying to talk me out of rocking your world in our car?"

With a hum, I urged her closer. "Thought you wanted a piggy-back ride?"

"It's a woman's prerogative to change her mind *or* to want two things at once. Even if they're physiologically impossible."

I had to laugh. "How many glasses of Champagne did you have?"

"Two."

"Liar."

"I did! I had designs on you, so I knew to limit the booze. You wouldn't fuck me the last time I got drunk. I asked nicely and everything."

"Don't pout. I like you fully aware of what I'm doing to you."

That earned me a shiver. "Don't remind me because if you say no to me tonight, I'll weep."

I pressed the lever on the driver's seat so it angled the backrest to a more comfortable position.

She squirreled closer then released a broken sigh when she wiggled and situated herself over the bulge in my pants. "You always tease me."

"Not always."

"Always." Her hips rolled. "Pretending like you're not hard for me—"

"I'm always hard for you. Whenever you come into a room, I have a semi."

"Is that true?" she asked gleefully.

"You can check if you want. Just not tomorrow."

Her laughter cascaded over me like bubbles from the Champagne she loved, but she fidgeted some more until her skirt was higher up her thighs.

"I'm sure you wear stuff like this to torment me."

"Of course. I love feeding your fantasies."

"You do that by breathing."

Despite the compliment, she tipped her head to the side. "You seem pensive tonight."

"Not at all." I smoothed my fingers over her upper thighs.

"You weren't like the others. Worried about your gift."

I shrugged then smirked when she popped out her bottom lip. "There are a handful of hours before Christmas morning."

"Maybe I want my gift now," she drawled, reaching between us and stroking my cock through my pants.

"Your gift is more than my dick."

"What did you get me?"

"Security."

"More coins?"

I toyed with one of her thigh-highs, enjoying her tremble as I swept higher, over her inner thigh. "Nope."

Whenever she graced me with a look this long, I felt her eyes bore into my soul. It laid me out before her. Blood and sinew and bones and a heart that beat for her alone.

I could tell she didn't believe me. That she thought her gift included a coin or two to join my first real gift to her, and maybe in the future, it would. Aidan had dumped a shit ton of work onto my shoulders recently, and I knew he intended to bombard me as we began to separate the Firm to whitewash Shay's background.

But her lips caught mine and thoughts of work swept away like driftwood on the shore. In her kiss, I knew she'd found whatever she'd sought.

Soft, tender pecks dotted over my mouth and chin and jaw. Spreading along my cheek and up to my ear, to my temple and the center of my forehead, where a furrow permanently resided.

When she rubbed her nose against mine, I relaxed back into the seat and groaned when the sound of the zipper retracting was overly loud in the silent car.

Gentle fingers retrieved me from within the folds of fabric, and I grunted as the tips danced over my length.

She shifted her feet, surging forward and up until she squatted over me. Sensing her hunger, I slid my hands over her inner thighs again and shifted the fabric of her panties aside.

My knuckles rubbed over her pussy along the way, earning the softest of mewls that deepened when I found her clit.

It was awkward and a tangle of limbs, but we made it work as I touched her and she held me until she brought us together—ass lowering and hand guiding me home.

I grunted as gravity did me the biggest of favors when her wet heat cosseted me from tip to midway down.

Camille licked her lips. "You know I'm never leaving you."

She said it so matter-of-factly that the words sank into my fucking nerve endings. The sharp jolt of pleasure I experienced had *her* moaning because my hips rocked, feeding another couple inches into the tight, hot clasp of her cunt.

"I like you to be safe." I panted, hands tugging on her ass and drawing her deeper into me so that she could perch on my knee. "I need you to be free. And I know you choose to stay with me when you have the tools to leave me."

It seemed obscene to have this discussion when she'd united us, but I knew she'd done it to keep me in place.

No way I'd avoid this conversation when she held my cock in her sweet, sweet pussy.

Her brow puckered. "And that makes you feel better?"

"It reminds me to be a husband worthy of you," I corrected, gritting my teeth as her inner muscles tormented me. "We all fuck up, and I know you wouldn't leave me over a dumb mistake I made..." Though her eyes turned into slits, I murmured, "If we go upstairs, I'll give you your gift now. We can even christen it."

"Christen a gift?!"

I nodded.

"Definitely not a coin then. Hmm... But how would we get there?" She tightened those torturous muscles even more. "You can't think I'll let go of you now that I have you."

The shudder that rushed down my spine at that claiming felt like the precursor to an orgasm.

"You always have me," I ground out.

"I know I do." She pressed a kiss to the tip of my nose this time. "I want to see my gift."

My lips twitched into a grin. "I know how to get you up there without your feet touching the ground."

"Did you turn into a magician when I wasn't looking?"

"Maybe." I grabbed the keys from the ignition, hissing as the shift in position had her clinging to me again as she resettled herself. "Hold these?"

She snagged them and tipped them between the deep V of her sweater dress. Seeing them peeking out of her bra was a fantasy I didn't even know I had.

My woman adorned in the keys of my favorite vintage car?

Fuck emeralds and diamonds, teenaged Brennan would have wept in delight.

I tugged on her skirt, pulling it down as far as our current situation would allow.

At her cocked brow, I answered, "So you don't get a draft up your ass."

Her eyes lit up with amusement. "Your dick too."

"You'll just need to make sure I don't get too soft then, won't you? Up to the task?"

Her muscles tightened again. "My Kegels are stronger than your biceps."

Snickering, I grabbed my cell and tapped onto one of Conor's apps that allowed me to check out the secure area. Seeing that all was well, I opened my door. The mellow warmth from the heated garage hit us both, but for whatever reason, it only seemed to amplify the heat where our bodies connected.

I swerved my legs out of the footwell, grabbed a hold of her ass, then did a visual of the parking garage before carefully surging into a standing position.

"You really are a magician," she praised breathily as I managed to get us out of the vehicle without falling on our asses.

A second glance around confirmed what I knew to be true—we were alone—but a man triple-checked when he held a treasure in his arms.

"Ready?"

She pushed her forehead against mine and moaned with each step I took. "FUCK," she bit off, her teeth finding my bottom lip as she tugged on it hard enough for them both to part and for her to slide her tongue in deep.

Camille fucked me there because she knew if she rolled her hips, that'd be game over—no way would I screw her in the parking lot when it was this open and not secure enough for my liking.

She delved between us to snag the keys and wafted the secure keychain at the elevator console. Once the doors opened, I herded us inside.

As soon as I pinned her to the wall, it was game over. My hips jerked back as I fucked my dick into her. Her delighted hiss had my eyes turning into slits.

"Feel good, baby?"

"You know it does." She whined, her pussy pulsing and fluttering around me.

I reached between us and ran my thumb around our joining. When I slipped that into her, she grunted and her spine arched at the sudden fullness. I rubbed against the thick vein along the back of my shaft, shifting inside her until she moaned.

Having uncovered that soft cluster of tissue that pleaded with me for more, I held my cock at the right angle to blow her mind.

Her breath soughed in and out of her chest as I moved slowly, enough that every thrust intentionally had the tip of my dick tormenting her G-spot.

Her eyes screwed up like she was in pain. "Brennan," she burst out, panting my name over and over like a litany. "Faster. Please. Fuck. Please. Oh, Brennan, I can't... I'm so—"

My hips deliberately slowed as, in the reflection, I caught sight of the floor we were on.

"No!" she howled, her hands grabbing my ears as the doors opened. "You do not fucking stop."

Delight and satisfaction and pure, primal euphoria at my mate, my woman, commanding her release, commanding *me* when no one else would dare, roared through me.

I stopped fucking around and just fucked her.

She keened and wailed and howled again as I pummeled her G-spot over and over. Each thrust, deep and fast, had her growing tenser until she was like a steel rod in my arms.

Then, she broke.

She cascaded.

She exploded.

A single, short, sharp scream rang in my ears as her pussy almost pushed me out, she clenched around me so hard. Then, her hands ripped and tore at my shoulders, the fabric ruined by her nails and her grip.

She looked tortured.

But I felt the truth in how her cunt detonated around me.

When I came, it was almost anticlimactic.

It was always good with Camille. Always a relief to fill her full of my cum again. To brand her inside and out.

But nothing beat that primitive pride at how I'd wrecked her.

Only me.

Only I got her.

Only I'd do this to her.

Only me.

She'd only ever let herself go with me.

And that truth was better than an orgasm.

I hissed as I pumped my seed into her, enjoying the way she sagged into me, utterly replete, utterly calm.

For endless moments, I just loomed over her. Catching my breath, enjoying the aftershocks, reveling in our proximity.

Then, it registered we were still in the goddamn elevator, and I heaved a sigh and straightened up.

Her legs were slack around me, so I slapped her outer thigh and she yelped.

"Don't let go."

Her dazed eyes ensnared mine. "Brennan?"

"Your gift, remember?"

"Nap first. Then gift. Then Finn and Aoife's."

I grinned. "Oh, no. You wanted to see it, and I always give you what you want, don't I, Camille?"

A whimper escaped her. "Yes, Brennan."

"Do you like what I give you?"

She stretched, luxuriously, languidly. "Always."

Unsurprised when she draped herself onto me, head propped on my shoulders, arms dangling over them too, I hit the "open doors" button before I moved away from the wall.

Thirty seconds later, we were home.

The silence was always a relief after a family get-together, and my ears rang with it.

"You know, when I was a kid, I'd never have said it was possible for us to be louder."

Camille stroked my jaw, her fingers lax. "The more the merrier."

"The more happy I am to get home," I corrected wryly, allowing the peace to saturate my eardrums. "I love them but fuck, they're a lot all at once." Leaving peace would be hard, but Roman would love Christmas morning with all his family around.

"They'll only get worse as we start having more kids."

I paused in the hall. "You have something to tell me, baby?"

She hesitated. Then, her pussy tightened around me when my cock grew hard.

I jerked my head backward so that I could stare at her, but her gaze turned shy.

"Don't hide from me," I warned, voice gruff.

Her throat bobbed. "Not yet."

"Oh?"

She shrugged. "Would it be so bad?"

"You know it wouldn't. I'd love Roman to have siblings. Hell, you can feel my reaction. More of you to love." Still, I studied her. "You nervous? Why aren't you looking at me?"

Sucking her top lip between her teeth, she nibbled on it. "I thought I was and I wasn't, and I got excited even though I'm still on the shot. Dumb—"

"Never dumb." I growled the words. "And if you want another of my babies, then fuck if we won't make that happen."

The idea of her round with my child again—Jesus.

She'd about killed me when she'd carried Roman. So fucking delicate, so fucking fragile, yet so fucking strong at the same time.

"Brennan," she said around a laugh that ended with a moan as my cock shifted from a semi to full, and I was too fucking old for that. "We can't—"

"Sure we can. When's your next doctor's appointment?"

Her eyes widened. "You really mean it?"

"Of course I do."

"Beginning of February."

"Then, cancel it."

Her breathing hitched. "Are we doing this again?!"

Delight filled me because she looked so fucking happy. "We are."

"I know it might take a while." Her brow furrowed. "My cycle has to regulate and—"

"It'll take however long it takes," I assured her. "We're in no rush, but we're definitely planning this, right?"

"Right." She beamed at me, then released a squeal as she tightened her arms around my neck. "I have the best husband in the world!"

I shook my head. "Oh, sweetheart, you don't, but I can only try."

"My opinion is the only one that counts. Nobody else's."

Because I could tell she was on the brink of turning militant and my dick couldn't have withstood that, I distracted her: "Ready to see your surprise?"

She nodded as I guided her toward one of the guest bedrooms. I'd honestly thought about getting rid of my pool room, but I had fond memories of that pool table and didn't intend on denying myself the thrill that came every game I played.

So, I'd sacrificed a guest room.

If that meant I couldn't have my whole family stay here, then boo hoo. They could fuck off to their own places.

Her brow furrowed as we hovered outside one of the doors. "This looks... different." She angled her head to the side and muttered, "Is that an AC controller?"

"No. It just looks like it." Pinning her to the wall, I tapped a button. The temperature controls faded. I pressed my finger to the touch screen and it scanned my retina. "Later, I'll add your details to this."

Her eyes widened but she nodded.

"Only you and I will be able to get in here."

Her mouth worked. "Is that necessary?"

"Safety. Security. My watch words with you."

"God, you and Eoghan," she grumbled, but she didn't look too upset.

I had to figure that Eoghan and I had lucked out on the wife department just for this alone—both of them knew what it was like for their homes to be infiltrated. They knew that safety was relative, so they didn't have a problem with us being security zealots.

When the door unlocked, I murmured, "Safe room. Reinforced walls—"

"Holy shit!" She twisted in my hold, which did interesting things down below. "This is why we've been at Eoghan's so much this week!"

"Long-term planning. He's not the only sneak."

"That isn't as reassuring as you think."

"This will hold until I can get to you, and if I can't, one of my brothers." I cupped her shoulder as I tried to condense my fears for the future without scaring her. "I'm not saying this to freak you out—"

"No. You're just telling me that I'm your priority." A gleam appeared in her eyes. "That is never not a compliment."

"Good to know." I smirked when, really, I was relieved I didn't have to sell the idea to her. "Ready?"

"God, yes."

I motioned at her to open the door, and she grabbed the handle now that it was unlocked.

Turning it, she peered around the corner then gasped. "Oh, my god!"

Striding into the room, I took in the work and had to admit, my crew and Inessa had done me a fucking solid.

The walls were a creamy pink, and the pale ash-blond office furniture had gold accents while the soft furnishings were cozy, but there were those box-type shelves that'd organize even the messiest of souls and that certainly wasn't my wife.

It was already filled with her knickknacks and a bunch of her yarn, as well as drawers and a shelving unit that Inessa told me would help her keep her crafts separated.

There was a play corner for Roman, as well as a large sofa that would convert into a bed. Just off the room, a small hall led to a tiny kitchen and bathroom area.

Not that the practicalities appealed to her.

But her and Roman's safety was *all* that mattered. Inessa had just prettied it up.

"Turn left," I ordered so that she faced the wall of books.

For an endless amount of time, she gawked at it then she squealed again, and her mouth collided with mine.

Proof I'd done good.

Confirmed when the barrage of kisses continued into multiple minutes of her showing me her appreciation for the gift that had been tailored to her.

Her nails dug into my throat as she angled my head back, and then she didn't just nip my bottom lip. She outright bit it. "Fuck a baby into me, Brennan O'Donnelly."

And that goddamn Neanderthal in me didn't give a shit about that conversation we'd just had. Didn't care that medicine would prevent it.

I just did as any Fecker would on Christmas Eve...

I gave my bride precisely what she asked of me.

SEVENTEEN
TEXT CHAT

Brennan: Erase all CCTV footage from my elevator/private parking for the past thirty minutes

Conor: Camille blessed you, huh?

Conor: Is this your Christmas gift?

Brennan: Fuck off

Conor: You owe me. Again.

Brennan: When don't I?

Conor: Where's my 'please' and 'thank you?'"

Brennan: At the bottom of the Hudson

EIGHTEEN

"PADDY, I've just gotten off a three-hour long Valentini gift-opening video call where all my nieces and nephews decided to surprise us with an off-key rendition of a horrendous Sicilian carol! I don't have time for this. I have three girls to get ready, and as far as I'm aware, you know how to dress yourself."

Not that you could tell from the heinous Christmas sweater he wore.

It looked like it had been made from the fur Pebbles's shed.

Watching me tug the rollers from my hair, he wailed, "But Lena's like you. She makes me dress right!"

"It isn't a crime. Luc said he bought you a capsule closet. That means everything matches everything else."

"Since when did blue and brown go together?"

"Since 2020."

He hissed out a breath and stared mournfully at the blue silk suit he'd hung on his bathroom door and the loafers Luc had paired with them.

Because he seemed completely lost, I sighed. "What is it, Dad?"

He peeped at me. "I want to look nice for her."

"And you will. Luc wouldn't steer you wrong." I glanced at my watch, hoping the gesture would distract him. "Thank you for this, by the way."

His shoulders straightened. "You like it?"

Relieved, I smiled at him. "I do." And I did.

I had a feeling Lena had helped him pick it out, but I'd take it—it was a very pretty, slimline Patek Philippe. But even better, it was vintage. I liked that it had character, and I liked even more that they'd both worked out that I'd changed.

The Jen of before had wanted everything shiny. I'd been a magpie for brands and designers. Now, I needed something else. Luciu had given me expensive tastes too.

"I'm glad, honey." His gaze softened. "What did that boy get you?"

"He's not a boy, Dad."

"He is to me!"

I tutted. "He bought me a yacht."

"Christ Almighty—a boat?! He bought you a boat?"

"A yacht," I corrected with a dry smile. "It's moored in Monaco. It's where we became *official*."

"Official? What's that supposed to mean?"

"Never you mind."

"So you haven't seen it?"

"Only pictures. We're in Catania."

"You're still okay with us coming, aren't you?"

"Of course. Just don't flirt with Lauren. I don't want to be tending to your cheeks when Luc and Stan cut them to shreds. You don't even want to know what Rory'll do to you."

"I'll be bringing Lena! Of course I wouldn't flirt in front of her. She'd have my balls, never mind my cheeks."

"I don't get why you like her so much. Not unless you're a masochist."

"A maso-what-now?"

"Like pain."

He rubbed his chin. "Like Evel Knievel?"

"No." I heaved a sigh. "Never mind. Look, is your fashion crisis over? Can I get onto clothing my babies for the day?!"

"You sure about the brown and blue?"

"Deadly."

He harrumphed.

"Did you call Liam?"

"He didn't pick up."

"What did you say to him now?" I chided. Honestly, having a half-brother and a father was such a pain in the ass. I didn't know how Luciu coped with *two* siblings.

"Nothing!"

"Liar."

"I'm not lying."

When he scratched his chin again, I drawled, "You need to shave. Lena will give you shit if you're scratching like you have fleas."

"I don't have fleas!"

"Well, stop scratching then." I folded my arms across my chest. "What did you say to Liam?"

"I didn't!" he protested. "I spoke to Gracie."

"So, she gave you shit on his behalf?"

"That one's got a nastier tongue on her than you do."

I smirked. "She definitely handed you your ass, huh?"

"Fi?!"

My head whipped to the side when Luc called. I held up a hand at my father to shut him up and yelled back, "Luc?"

A flurry of Sicilian came next, so I heaved an impatient sigh and pointed at the screen. "Blue and brown look good together. I think Lena will appreciate your slutty, little new specs so wear them too—"

"My slutty-what-now?! Why aren't you speaking English today? Too long in Sicily, that's what—"

"Bye, Dad!" I cut him off before I got a lecture about how I should stay in the city where it was safe.

Safe.

Right.

Leaving my cell on the vanity in my dressing room, I darted into the bedroom where Luc stood—

"For God's sake. What the hell were you thinking?" I bustled over to him and yanked on his hand until I could guide him into the bathroom. "I told you not to use the coal!"

"It's tradition! They have to learn about *La Befana!*"

"It isn't even Epiphany yet," I chided as I wiped his face clean of coal dust. "And do I even want to know how this happened?"

"Saverina happened. She ran into the backs of my legs. Down I went."

"Don't pout," I grumbled, grabbing my makeup wipes and using one to cleanse his face. "I'm the one who should be pouting! My husband's covered in three-million-year-old fossil dust and trying to terrify our children into thinking that a witch will judge whether they've been naughty or nice."

"She isn't a witch. I never thought she was. She just chose not to go with the Three Wise Men!"

"Your mother says she's a witch. If you want to argue with her, I'll be there in ringside seats. Until then, why did our daughter attack you?"

"Saverina tried to sneak out. I caught her dressed in a swimsuit—"

My eyes widened in horror. "She wanted to go swimming?!"

"Said it wasn't fair that we were making her wear a dress when she wanted to be a mermaid." His lips twitched. "If she hadn't scared the shit out of me, I'd have laughed. She made a tail out of toilet paper roll."

"It isn't funny!" I said around a laugh of my own. "She didn't think the toilet paper would get wet?"

"She said Ursula would make it real."

"Ah, fuck." I'd done too good a job of making my daughter love the Disney villains. "It's going to be one of those days, isn't it? Where is she now?"

"With *Matri.*"

"And Lauren was in on the *La Befana* preview, was she?"

"Not exactly." He rested his head on the swell of my stomach. "Please, God, let this be a boy."

I stroked my fingers through his hair, uncaring that he was dirtying my white robe. "Your sperm makes the best girl babies."

He moaned pitifully. "It really does."

NINETEEN

I FLICKED Paddy's forehead when he got too close to me and I knew he was angling for a kiss. Instead, I chivvied, "Did you brush your teeth? I'm not having my first transatlantic Christmas gift opening with you and spinach stuck between them."

Paddy complained, "It was one time, Lena! You're such a hard ass."

"Like you don't need some bossing around." I sniffed. And I meant it. "It's a shame Liam couldn't make it today."

"Nah, he hangs around with the Bukowskis come the holidays." He pulled a face that spoke of resignation and wistful longing. "Fucked up with both my kids."

"It's an O'Donnelly trait I'm hoping this generation breaks," I said wryly.

"Me too."

"Have you heard from Jennifer?"

"She video-called. Loved her watch." He nudged me. "Thank you for helping me pick out their gifts. Meant a lot."

"Don't be silly. It's fine." I refused to blush.

"You sure you're okay with ending the trip in Sicily?"

"Of course I am. Seeing in the new year there sounds wonderful. They don't mind *me* coming to their villa, do they?"

"Wouldn't have invited us if they did."

"It'll just be them?"

He nodded. "They don't all leave the country at once."

I huffed but I understood the necessity, even if I was sick of it.

A lifetime of abiding by bylaws that the rest of the world never even imagined existed was incredibly wearing on one's patience.

"Now, how do I look?"

"Surprisingly casual." I felt his eyes on me. "You're still a looker, Magdalena."

My lips curved. "I know." Then, I turned to him and conceded, "When you shave, brush your teeth, and make sure to wear the clothes Luciu bought you, you're a looker too, Padraig."

He puffed up, just like I knew he would. "Right, shall I start the call?"

We were six hours ahead of New York right now, so that meant the family had probably gathered at Aoife and Finn's, gifts would be opened soon, and lunch had yet to be served.

"You're not wearing your glasses," I snapped when he squinted at the screen. "Put the damn things on. I bought you that chain to use around your neck. Why don't you wear it?"

"Because it feels like it's choking me!"

"I'll choke you if I see you squint at that phone again. Wear your damn glasses!"

"Ma, are you giving Uncle Paddy a hard time?" my eldest greeted.

"Hopefully, he's giving *her* something hard—"

"Star! Jesus Christ," Conor yelped.

"You eejit, Padraig. You hit connect!" I snatched the phone and ordered, "Get your glasses or you won't be able to see anything." To Aidan, I complained, "Four days I've had to put up with this one and his refusal to wear glasses. What on earth did he buy them for if he won't wear them?"

"Because they make my eyes ache!"

"Because you haven't worn them enough." I studied him now that he'd put the frames on. "You look very dapper, Paddy."

His eyes widened. "I do? Well, if you like them, I'll make sure they're glued to my face."

"Should have told him that before, Ma. He'll wear them in the shower now."

Ignoring my eldest and refusing to admit that both Paddy and I were blushing like Shay did whenever Kat smiled at him, I remarked, "You do, Padraig. And I can tell you now that you don't when you scrunch your face up at the screen."

Conor snorted. "Ma, cut the man some slack. It's Christmas Day!"

"I'll cut him some slack when he's dead. He chose to come with me, you know? That means he likes it when I'm mean to him."

I heard Star chortle in the back. "Bring it on, Lena. Show him who's boss."

The two of us didn't always get along, but sometimes we held similar opinions.

When she peered over Aidan's shoulder, I asked, "Now, what's this about me giving someone something hard?"

Aidan spewed out his drink. "Ma!"

I blinked. "What?!"

"Oh, my god." Conor groaned.

With a suspiciously wicked grin on her face, Star grabbed the phone. "Don't worry. You won't have to talk to me for long. I'm just setting up the projector."

"We're going to be on the big screen?" I asked in excitement.

"Easiest way for you to see what's going on. If the call disconnects, don't worry. I'll call back."

"Why are my boys in the middle of conniption fits?"

"Because males are the emotional sex, Lena, why else?"

Because we agreed about that too, I simply peered around her when I saw someone bounce into shot and squealed, "Cameron! How's my boy?!"

"I thought *I* was your boy, Ma," Brennan drawled over on the sofa with Camille, of course.

I swore those two were stitched together at the hip. But I wasn't complaining. A part of me remembered the days when Aidan and I had been like that. A few inches between us had been a few too many.

During the holidays, I missed him like my heart had been cut from my chest.

There'd be no more sneaky kisses under the mistletoe or finding gifts dotted around the house before Christmas. No fidgety hand to hold in church or corn anything to make for the fiend...

But I had my children.

And, maybe, Paddy.

And all my glorious grandbabies.

Now, if only Inessa would add to the pile, I'd die a happy woman.

My smile turned wistful. "You're always my boy."

"What about us?" Declan and Eoghan chimed in.

"Oh, hush, the lot of you. I loved my gifts, by the way. I can't believe you remembered I love *Capodimante.* It's years since I bought any." Tears pricked my eyes at their thoughtfulness. "Now, what time are we opening presents?"

Aoife caught my eye and, timidly, I smiled at her. She smiled back, and a world of hurt shone back at me.

I was to blame for that.

So many sins I'd committed against that girl, and while some should have put me in a cell, I thought the worst was the rupture of our own relationship.

I still thought of her as my daughter, even if she hated my guts.

When she ducked away, I didn't comment and nobody else did

either. Another sin—I'd done this. Brought this tension to the family. A tension that was impossible to heal.

It was why I'd agreed to this 'vacation.'

Aoife deserved to host the holiday meal without stressing about what to do with the problem that was *me.*

Eventually, Star disappeared and Conor took her place as they both fiddled around with whatever they'd done to the TV.

"Did Alessa manage to come?" I asked.

"No. Stomach flu's swept through the Sinners' compound," Conor answered, glancing up from a screen.

My Aidan would have been rolling around in his grave if he knew we were breaking bread on Christmas Day itself with some bikers, but... it wasn't his time anymore.

It was our sons'.

Aidan poured some whiskey into a glass then made a toast. "Thanks for this, boys. I'd offer you some, but it's wasted on your plebeian tongues."

"Don't worry. I can cut his out now that you got me my Damascus," Eoghan drawled.

"Eoghan," I reprimanded. "What's a Damascus?"

"A special knife, Ma," he chirped.

"How special?"

"Six-hundred plus layers of Damascus steel and the handle's made from five-thousand-year-old bog oak—"

"That's also a kitchen knife," Finn drawled. "Not for slitting throats."

"Finn!" Aoife chided. "Not in front of the kids."

"They're not interested." He wafted a hand at the tree and the chaos of so many of our babies tussling over whose gift was whose.

"What did they get you?" I asked him gingerly.

Relieved he didn't blank me, I gave him a soft smile when he answered, "A tie pin."

"Only because you're so fucking hard to buy for," Declan groused.

"I told you what I wanted."

"We weren't buying you a data center for Christmas, Finn. You need a better work/life balance," Conor derided as he stole the whiskey tumbler from Aidan's hand. "And if I'm saying that, you know you have issues."

"I want to destroy it—"

"We can do that in the New Year." Conor tutted, then *sotto voce*, he added, "We talked about this—"

"And you, son?" I interrupted before they could get all technical on me. "What did they get you?"

Conor grinned. "*Donkey Kong*. The arcade game."

"And you, Dec?" Paddy called out.

"Oh, a Degas charcoal."

"A Digga who now?"

Declan heaved a sigh. "Never mind. What did you get Liam?"

Paddy's nose scrunched. "He won't take gifts from me."

"That doesn't mean you stop trying." Conor tutted. "You better not have fucked with his mojo, Paddy. We have a cup to win this year."

"It's never too late to try, Paddy," Aoife offered gently, but her gaze glanced off me and she scuttled into the kitchen again.

My heart clenched, hope shimmering through it, but I shifted focus as Paddy huffed. "Liam doesn't need me."

"We always need our dad," Aidan corrected, a frown on his face.

"Even if he's a fuckup," Eoghan agreed, his tone grim.

"Jesus, what the hell happened here?" Star complained. "I left and you were laughing and giving Aidan shit for his bougie taste in liquors! Now it's like we're at a crime scene."

I pulled a face but couldn't deny she was right.

Clapping my hands together, I declared, "Time to gather around the tree, everyone."

My words, even from across the pond, transmitted wide and far. I beamed at my boys and their girls as they settled around the tree while the children laughed and shrieked and played.

"Such a beautiful sight," I praised. "Oh! Where's Victoria?"

Camille cleared her throat. "She'll be here for lunch."

Shay snorted. "Yeah, right."

"Leave it," Eoghan ordered.

My eyes widened at his tone, but even as I wondered why he'd sounded like that, I pivoted: "Gifts! I want to see this Secret Santa malarkey first."

"I apologize in advance to the person who got my present," Savannah chimed in glumly until Aidan pressed a kiss to her lips to shut her up.

"I don't," Star muttered.

"Or me. Mine took me ages," Aela said dryly.

Camille shrugged. "Mine turned out all right."

"And mine."

Star tossed a pillow at Aoife. "Of course it did, Ms. Home Shit Queen."

"Star, must you swear?" I chided.

"Don't discourage her, Grandma Lena! I'm collecting!" Kat yelled.

"Still?"

"Hey, we're funding a sanctuary on Star's sailor mouth," Eoghan drawled. "Don't stop her, Ma."

With another tut, I prodded, "Well, get on with it! I want to see what you came up with."

Star tossed a package onto Aoife's knee. "You're welcome. And if you ever sell them to your home-goods empire, I want a forty per cent cut."

Aoife narrowed her eyes. "Thirty."

"Good girl," Finn crooned.

Conor elbowed Star. "Thirty-eight."

"Thirty-one."

"Thirty-seven-point-five."

"Thirty-one-point-five."

"You don't even know what I'm taking a cut of yet!"

She shrugged. "You're too smug for it to be shit."

"Kat! Aunt Aoife owes you ten bucks, too."

"Thanks, Aunt Aoife!" Kat hollered over from the other side of the room, where the kids were tearing into their gifts like the heathens they could be when they got together.

Even Shay, who was "too cool" for anything these days, tore through wrapping paper like that fellow with the scissors on his hands.

Aoife carefully unfolded the tucks on her own gift until Star sighed. "Just rip it."

"It's my gift!" Aoife snapped, but she finally uncovered a box.

I was surprised but grateful when she held it up to me, though I had no idea what it was.

Star beamed at her. "My extra-loud crackers."

"Bombs," Conor muttered.

"They're not bombs. How many times? I've made bombs, dammit. I know the difference."

Aoife stared at them with a frown. "Are they going to take off my hands?"

"No!" Huffing, Star leaned over, grabbed one of the oddly shaped things, and waggled it when Aoife didn't bite. "Go on!"

Finn snagged the cracker. "If you take off a finger, I'll bill you for it."

"I'll see you in court first," she derided, but she pulled the end of her side.

"Holy mother of God!" I yelled over the resulting bang. "What in Mother Mary's name was that?!"

Star, ignoring me, demanded shrilly, "See why I want forty percent?!"

Glitter as well as tiny pieces of confetti drenched Aoife, Finn, and Star. Never mind the rest of the room! Even the children stopped squawking to figure out what had caused such a racket.

None cried, of course.

My Aidan would be so proud.

As for Baby Aidan, sensing her favorite brand of mischief, she toddled over to her mother's side to investigate and tugged on Savannah's skirt. My eldest plunked her onto his lap instead so she could watch the chaos from a better angle.

Finn yanked on his ear. "That really is a lawsuit waiting to happen."

"Maybe it needs tweaking," Aoife whisper-shouted. "But the reach is impressive. Thirty-three-point-five."

"Aoife!"

"They'd be great on July 4th, Finn," she yelled back.

Aela swept in, hands wafting through the still-falling glitter. "I'm confiscating these. Someone has to be the responsible adult."

"Thirty-six," Star hollered. "Final offer!"

Aoife stuck out her hand. "Fine."

As they shook on it, I tsked—these girls were all work, work, work.

Aoife nudged Finn with her elbow. "Pass me mine, please?"

"Damn, they're loud," Paddy grumbled, tugging on his own ear. "Can you turn down the phone?"

"Stop whining." But I did as he said because they were definitely shouting.

"Aela, I know you talked about missing the Irish kind so I found a recipe." Aoife beamed at her. "I hope you enjoy it."

Aela, frowning, unwrapped the tin and then pulled off the lid to reveal a cake frosted in royal icing.

Beneath the frosting, there was a layer of yellow stuff that I recognized as marzipan and then a dense fruit cake.

Paddy whistled. "That looks like mighty fine Christmas cake, Aoife. Wish I were there to eat it. My grandmother used to bake that every year. She'd soak it in brandy too."

"I did that," Aoife shouted back. "Fed it a couple times. I also made one that's kiddo approved."

Aela pressed a hand to her mouth. "Aoife, you didn't have to—"

"Sure I did! As soon as I picked your name, I knew this would work out perfectly. You miss the stuff you had back there."

Aela's smile trembled. "You're the best."

Camille pressed what appeared to be an extra-large book into Star's hands.

Star frowned at it, then at Camille, but despite how she ragged Aoife, gently unwrapped the present. Her eyes widened and she gasped once she set eyes on it.

"What did Camille get you?" Paddy demanded.

Star's voice sounded surprisingly thick. "It's a scrapbook. Of my parents and Dad on tour."

Camille cleared her throat. "Savannah helped me and so did her mom and dad."

Gentle fingers tripped over the images within the bound book and she breathed, "Wow."

"I didn't mean to upset you," Camille mumbled a touch awkwardly.

Tear-drenched eyes caught Camille's, right before Star hurled herself at the younger woman. Beavis and Butthead, Conor's dogs, immediately leapt into the chaos, but Star didn't stop them as they tried to lick her face once she released Camille from her hug. If anything, she hid in Butthead's fur.

Even Conor looked surprised at the outburst, but I found Camille was the best prepared for emotional explosions.

While they were otherwise occupied, Aela grinned at Savannah and handed her a box. "There you go, Savvie."

My eldest's wife beamed and tore open the wrapping paper on the thin but somehow fat box. Savannah gasped. "Aela, it's beautiful!"

She tilted the gift to reveal a glass-blown ornament—a "3."

"It's *meeeeeeee*," Aidan squeaked, and her father had to hold her hands to stop her from toying with the delicate ornament.

"I remember when I had a tree full of Aela original decs," Conor muttered with a gimlet stare at Shay, whose shoulders hunched.

"Sorry, Uncle Con."

Ignoring them all and shaping the ornament's curlicues and fancy additions with a delicate touch, Savannah sighed happily. "I love it. Thank you, Aela."

I tutted. "I still don't agree with calling a little girl 'Third.'"

"Good thing it has nothing to do with you, Ma," my eldest intoned with a narrow-eyed look. "If I'm a Jr. in my goddamn forties, then she can be an Aidan III as a little girl."

"Yeah, don't be sexist, Nana," Shay rebuked.

"Shay!"

"What? It's true! You said it yourself. 'A little girl' shouldn't be called Third. So if Aidan were a boy, it'd be okay?"

I knew it wasn't fair, but I still glowered at Katina. Ever since she'd wrapped my boy around her finger, he'd grown even more outspoken!

"She's so delicate—"

Inessa coughed and I immediately let the subject drop. After my dinner, I didn't want to rile up Eoghan again.

"Camille?"

Surprisingly, Star was still tucked into Camille's side, gently peeling past the paper that separated the pages to reveal pockets of memories from her childhood.

"Nessie?"

"I hope you liked your office?"

Camille blinked then beamed at her baby sister. "I should have known you two were plotting behind my back!"

Brennan couldn't have looked smugger if he tried, and Inessa blushed. "We can change it—"

"No way! I adore it! Thank you," Camille breathed. "It's beautiful."

"What happened?" I insisted, utterly in the dark. "What office?"

"I decorated Camille's new office," Inessa answered, flicking me a smile. "I overheard Brennan and Eoghan discussing safe rooms." She rolled her eyes. "So I got involved or Camille would have been greeted with concrete walls and steel bars!"

"Makes sense," I informed Paddy as Camille began itemizing every single thing she adored about the gift. "She's studying it, you know?"

"Studying what?"

"Interior design. She'll be graduating in the spring." Because he looked like I'd switched into Gaelic, I sighed. "It's where you decorate— You know what? Never mind."

I returned my focus to Savannah.

Her gift intrigued me. Crocheting hadn't come easily to the girl, but before I'd left for Europe, she'd been able to regulate her tension and at least follow a pattern.

Savannah sucked in a breath. "Okay. My turn to get this over with." She snagged the package and, with a shyness I didn't think she had in her, passed the gift to Inessa.

Inessa cautiously opened the package and then her brow furrowed. "Are these.... crocheted underwear?"

Savannah bit her lip, then a hangnail, then her lip again. "They're for your books."

"What?"

"You know. Bookmarks."

Her mouth opened. "Bookmarks?"

"But they look like underwear." Savannah's laughter sounded weak even thousands of miles away. "You know... a joke? You put the thong between the page and it marks your place."

Inessa glanced at the surprisingly well-done *thing* then burst out laughing. Savannah flinched, Aidan tensed up, prickly like a pissed-off tiger whenever his mate was agitated, then Inessa cheered, "I fucking love it!"

"Inessa, you owe me ten bucks too!"

As the family cascaded into laughter at Kat's demand, Paddy and I shared a smile.

No, I didn't have Aidan anymore. And if he was watching over me, then he'd just have to endure watching his brother and I grow close.

He shouldn't have left me.

If Paddy's arm slipped around my shoulders and I relaxed into his side as I watched the rest of the gifts being opened, and I devoured the sight of my settled boys, the happiness they'd found despite their heritage, then it was nobody's business but our own.

And certainly not Aidan O'Donnelly Sr.'s.

TWENTY

SORRY, *Aidan, but Lena's mine now...*

THE END.

OR IS IT...

Maxim and Victoria's story is coming very, very soon... As is Stan's.
Watch this space!

AFTERWORD

Happy holidays, honey.

I hope you loved this slice of life from the O'Donnellys.

If you loved the ornament on the front cover of the book, you can purchase that on my website. Many of my series also have ornaments!

If you need some more Christmas with the fam, then check out LODESTAR. While it *is* Filthy Lies and Filthy Truth compiled together, at the end, there's a bonus story with lots of goodies. It's free to read in KU!

Watch this space for updates on when Stan and Maxim will be getting their stories.

Alternatively, make sure you never miss any news from me by signing up to my newsletter:

www.serenaakeroyd.com/newsletter

I also have a Patreon now where I actually wrote this story and uploaded it scene by scene. Be sure to check that out if it sounds like your cup of tea! www.patreon.com/serenaakeroydgamazurke

It's there where you will find a bonus scene once this story hits 500 reviews! It won't be behind a paywall but you will have to become a free member to access it.

You can always find me in my Diva reader group too: www.face
book.com/groups/SerenaAkeroydsDivas
Much love to you!
Serena
xo

THE CROSSOVER READING ORDER WITH THE SINNERS & VALENTINIS

FILTHY
FILTHY SINNER
NYX
LINK
FILTHY RICH
SIN
STEEL
FILTHY DARK
CRUZ
MAVERICK
FILTHY SEX
HAWK
FILTHY HOT
STORM
THE DON
THE LADY
FILTHY SECRET
REX
RACHEL

<u>FILTHY KING</u>
<u>FILTHY DISCIPLE</u>
<u>THE CONSIGLIERE</u>
<u>THE ORACLE</u>
<u>LODESTAR</u>
<u>SILENCED</u>
<u>END GAME</u>
WAITING GAME
THINGS LEFT UNSAID
COME BACK TO ME
>> FILTHY CHRISTMAS <<
<u>FILTHY RICHER</u>

CONNECT WITH SERENA

For the latest updates, be sure to check out my website!
But if you'd like to hang out with me and get to know me better, then
I'd love to see you in my Diva reader's group where you can find out
all the gossip on new releases as and when they happen. You can join
here: www.facebook.com/groups/SerenaAkeroydsDivas. Or you can
always PM or email me. I love to hear from you guys:
serenaakeroyd@gmail.com.

ABOUT THE AUTHOR

I'm a romance novelaholic and I won't touch a book unless I know there's a happy ending. This addiction is what made me craft stories that suit my voracious need for raunchy romance. I love twists and unexpected turns, and my novels all contain sexy guys, dark humor, and hot AF love scenes.

I write MF, menage, and reverse harem (also known as why choose romance,) in both contemporary and paranormal. Some of my stories are darker than others, but I can promise you one thing, you will always get the happy ending your heart needs!

9 781836 580331